D0455455

THE
HIDDEN
LAW

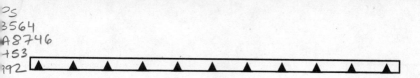

THE
HIDDEN
LAW

MICHAEL NAVA

HarperCollins*Publishers*

HarperCollins books may be purchased for educational, business, or sales promotional use. For information, please write: Special Markets Department, HarperCollins Publishers, Inc., 10 East 53rd Street, New York, NY 10022.

FIRST EDITION

Designed by Claudyne Bianco

Library of Congress Cataloging-in-Publication Data

Nava, Michael.
  The hidden law / Michael Nava.
    p. cm.
  ISBN 0-06-016783-1
  I. Title.
PS3564.A8746H53   1992
813'.54—dc20   91-58356

92 93 94 95 96 ❖/HC 10 9 8 7 6 5 4 3 2 1

For Joseph Hansen

ACKNOWLEDGMENTS

I want to thank Rob Miller, Dale and
Sharon Flanagan, and Katherine V. Forrest
for their friendship, support, and assistance,
and Andy Ferrero.

The Hidden Law does not deny
    Our laws of probability,
But takes the atom and the star
And human beings as they are
And answers nothing when we lie. . . .
Its utter patience will not try
To stop us if we want to die:
When we escape It in a car
When we forget It in a bar
These are the ways we're punished by
    The Hidden Law.

W. H. Auden
"The Hidden Law"

THE
HIDDEN
LAW

▲

CHAPTER

ONE

▼

I STOOD ON THE SIDEWALK IN FRONT OF CITY HALL IN DOWNTOWN LOS Angeles on a warm April morning thinking of my father, who had been dead for a long time, and "Dragnet," his favorite TV series. City Hall was engraved on the badge that Sergeant Friday flashed weekly in his dour pursuit of law and order, and my father never missed a single episode. He was a big believer in law and order. "Dragnet" fueled his black-and-white vision of the world as consisting of humorless machos like Sergeant Friday and himself battling the forces of evil. In my father's expansive view this included most Anglos, all blacks, many Mexicans, priests, Jews, lawyers, doctors, people on welfare, the rich, and everyone under forty. He was a great and impartial hater; anyone different from him became an object of his contempt. Homosexuals, had he allowed that such creatures existed, would certainly have qualified.

As I started up the steps to City Hall I wondered whether my father would have hated me more because I was homosexual or a lawyer. Then I reminded myself that he had never needed a reason to hate me. It was enough that I was not him. For my own part, I no longer hated my father, though, admittedly, this had become easier after his death. Forgiveness was still a problem.

I took the steps too fast and stopped to catch my breath when I reached the top. I was forty, and I found myself thinking of my father more often now than in all the years since his death. He was ferociously alive in my memory where all the old battles still raged on. Sometimes I had to remind myself not only that he was dead, but that I had been there. He had died in a brightly lit hospital room, slapping away my consoling hand and screaming at my mother, *"Mas luz, mas luz."* It had never been clear to me whether he was asking for more light, or crying out in fear at a light he perceived that the rest of us could not see. He had died with that mystery, as with so many others.

I entered the rotunda of City Hall, a grave, shadowy place, its walls made of great blocks of limestone. Three limp flags hung high above a circular floor of inlaid marble that depicted a Spanish galleon. Around the domed ceiling were eight figures in tile representing the attributes of municipal government: Public Service, Health, Trust, Art, Protection, Education, Law, and Government. I searched in vain for the other four: Expedience, Incompetence, Corruption, and Avarice. Undoubtedly I would encounter them in the hearing I was there to attend.

Six weeks earlier a bill had been introduced in the state senate by Senator Agustin Peña who represented East Los Angeles. Peña's bill made it a crime to "actively participate in any criminal street gang with knowledge that its members engage or have engaged in a pattern of criminal gang activity." Despite its abridgment of the First Amendment right to free association, the bill had been expected to clear the legislature easily. Even though passage was a foregone conclusion, the senate committee before whom the bill was pending had scheduled a public hearing in Los Angeles.

The committee's motives became clear when a *Los Angeles Times* columnist pointed out that the date of the hearing was also the last day for mayoral candidates to file for the upcoming June primary. The columnist cynically concluded that Senator Peña planned to use the occasion to announce his entry into the race, positioning himself as the law-and-order candidate. When asked about it, Peña, who had been preparing for months to run, coyly declined comment.

A few days later, in mid-March, Peña ran over an old man in Sacramento, killing him. At the time, the Senator's blood alcohol level was twice the legal limit for drunk driving. He was charged with gross vehicular manslaughter. Immediately thereafter, he had entered a drug-and-alcohol rehab called SafeHouse, and had not been heard from since. Two days ago, his office had announced that Peña would be appearing at the hearing to make a statement.

The hearing had become the hottest ticket in town. I entered the city council chamber, where the hearing was being held to a packed house. The Minicams were out in force representing TV stations as far north as San Francisco. Their presence reminded me that Peña was more than simply a local politician. He was perhaps the ranking Latino officeholder in the state, a symbol of the political aspirations of millions and, until his accident, the person most likely to become the first mayor of Los Angeles of Mexican descent in a hundred and fifty years.

Although I had met Peña occasionally over the years, most of what I knew about him came from his campaign brochures and the newspapers. The former still portrayed him as the lean idealist who had marched in the dust of Delano with Cesar Chavez a quarter-century earlier. In the latter, he was depicted as a powerful patronage politician. Both accounts agreed that he was effective at his job. Over the years, however, he had become in a vague but unmistakable manner tainted by his success, careless about appearances, arrogant in the pursuit of his objectives. The work shirts and jeans had given way to expensive suits tailored to conceal the growing thickness of his body. From my perspective he was no worse than most politicians, but certainly no better and I might even have voted for him.

Whether I would've voted for him or not, I thought his bill was a disaster and I had come to testify against it. As far as I was concerned, it was a mandate for police harassment in Latino and black communities, not that the cops needed much encouragement on that front. Only last year, members of the LAPD had been inadvertently videotaped as they pulled a black man out of his car and beat him senseless. His crime was failing to pull over with sufficient dispatch to receive a speeding ticket. The spin doctors in the department asserted "isolated incident," but my clients had been telling me for years about being beaten for what defense lawyers called contempt of cop. I didn't think it was a good idea to turn them loose on every poor black or Latino kid who gave them attitude. I had written a piece for the *Times* to that effect, and I was still getting hate calls three weeks later.

"Rios."

I glanced over my shoulder. Tomas Ochoa lumbered toward me. He was tall, big-gutted and deliberately graceless as he clomped across the floor, forcing people out of his way. He came up to me like an old friend, crowding the space between us. It was a trick he used on people shorter than himself to force them to look up when they spoke to him. I moved back a step.

Salt-and-pepper hair framed his dark moustached face. His eyes were hidden behind tinted aviator glasses. Ochoa preached the revolution from a classroom podium at the local state college where he taught in the Chicano Studies Department. On the wall of his office was a yellowing poster that demanded the end to the Anglo occupation of California.

The last time I had seen him was at his school where we had been on a panel discussing the spread of AIDS among the city's minorities. While the rest of us deplored the indifference with which minority political leaders had responded to the presence of

AIDS among their constituents, Ochoa took the position that it only affected elements of the minority communities which they were better off without, homosexuals and drug users. We had not parted on friendly terms.

I was surprised that he had sought me out today.

I said, "Hello, Tomas."

"I read your article in the *Times*," he said. "Where you defended the gangs."

"I didn't defend the gangs," I replied. "All I said was that there are better ways of dealing with them than turning the police loose."

"Listen, Rios, the gangs are the best thing that ever came out of the barrio. With a little political education, they could be urban guerrillas."

"I deal with gang members all the time," I told him. "They're not revolutionaries. They're drugged-out losers who get a little self-esteem by shooting each other."

He frowned at me. "So your solution is to plea-bargain them into prison."

"The solution has to start long before they reach me."

"The solution," he said, raising his voice, "is outside the system that you represent."

A few people had stopped to stare. I answered quietly, "The only thing I represent is my clients, Tomas, and I do it well."

"You represent something a lot worse than that," he said, jabbing a finger at me.

"Well, according to you, AIDS will take care of that," I replied. "Or would you prefer concentration camps like Castro? Or Hitler?"

"Take your choice," he said, moving away.

I watched him disappear into the sea of brown and black faces in the room, with the depressing certainty that he spoke for most of them. Whatever their other disagreements, the races all united in their contempt for people of my kind. The revolution never extended to matters of personal morality.

*   *   *

At the front of the room, the senators had begun to assemble. I found a seat just as the chairwoman of the committee called the hearing to order. Spruce and intricately-coiffed, she announced, "These hearings have been called for the purpose of encouraging public debate on SB 22, introduced by Senator Peña of East Los Angeles."

She was interrupted by a rising commotion from the audience as a door opened behind her and Agustin Peña walked briskly forward, the Minicams sweeping toward him. An aide pulled out his chair and he sat down, saying, "I apologize to the committee for my tardiness. I'd like to make a statement."

The presiding senator replied, "Certainly, Senator Peña. Welcome back."

"Thank you," he said. He raised his hand back over his shoulder. His aide handed him a sheaf of papers. Peña laid them on the desk before him and, for a moment, simply looked out at the crowd thoughtfully. His thick, black hair was brushed back from a long, narrow face that El Greco might have painted, strong and melancholy; it was the face of a man who had passed through something difficult and was not yet certain of his ground. He cleared his voice, and began to read from his papers.

"The streets of our poorest communities have become battlefields."

Nearby, someone whispered, audibly, "Yeah, they're full of drunk drivers."

"It's time for action," Peña continued. "It's time to send a message to the gangsters that the decent people of our cities will not tolerate—"

The same wag quipped, "Intoxicated politicians." But this time, someone shushed him.

"Their guns and their drugs," Peña concluded.

The crowd shifted restlessly waiting for him to address the topic of his political future. At length, he finished with his prepared statement and said, "Now, with the committee's indulgence I would like to address my constituents in the room on another matter."

The room began buzzing again and was gaveled to order, the presiding senator saying, "You have the floor, Gus."

"Thank you, Charlene," he said. "You've been a good friend to me. In the past two months I've had a chance to see, truly, who my real friends are. I'm gonna ask some people to come up here and join me: my wife, Graciela, and my children; my son, Tino, and my beautiful daughter, Angela."

The three got up from the front row and walked awkwardly to the dais where the senators were seated. His wife was a plump, pretty woman, who wore a photogenic dress of red and blue silk. She had mastered that vaguely beatific expression that Nancy Reagan had popularized among the wives of public figures. His teenage daughter kissed her father quickly and retreated to the background. His handsome son also kissed his father but remained at his side.

Peña, reaching for his wife's hand as he rose from his seat, said, "This is what life is really about, a loving family, people who stand by you no matter what, and these are the people I know I hurt the most with my alcoholism."

He paused for effect, and got it, the cameras clicking, the crowd whispering. I watched his family. His wife's mouth twitched but her expression did not change. The girl retreated farther back. The boy looked straight ahead. Now that he was on his feet, Peña was as relaxed as a talk show host working the crowd.

"I know that some of you in the press expected me to be making a different kind of announcement today, and I would be lying if I didn't tell you I would rather be standing here announcing my candidacy for mayor than admitting that I'm an alcoholic. Still," he smiled, "you roll with the punches." The back room echoes of that remark were more authentic than what came next. "But maybe by doing this, I can help someone else. All I can say is that I have had to look at my human weakness right in the eye and realize that I have spent so much time caring about and worrying about others, that I have not worried or cared enough about myself. I now know that it's time for me to take care of me, to accept my responsibilities and my weaknesses. But I say to others who are as pained and hurt as myself," and here he draped an arm over his son's shoulders while gripping his wife's hand, "I say to you, 'Join me brothers and sisters. We can make it. We will make it. It's going to be a lonely journey, but I stand and God stands with me.'"

He released his children and his wife. "As you know, I have been at an alcohol rehabilitation center, and I believe that I have been cured of this disease of alcoholism. I have begun to heal my body and my soul."

Looking at the camera rather than her husband, his wife said, "Gus, for you to admit you have this problem and to deal with it has truly lifted a burden from our souls." She gestured vaguely toward the children. "I thank God you have had the strength to realize that you are truly in God's hands. I know for our family this is just a beginning and we, Tino, Angela, and me, we will be with you every step of the way."

"God bless you, Graciela," he said, choking back tears. To my astonishment, people around me were also crying.

The presiding senator hammered the table with her gavel and said, "The committee stands in recess for fifteen minutes."

The media descended on the Peñas, who were soon obscured by flashing cameras and shouted questions. An old gray-haired woman sitting near me cast a skeptical eye on the scene and muttered to no one in particular, in Spanish, "The man has no shame."

The cameras were gone when the hearing was called back to order, as was Peña's family, and the proceeding reverted to its original purpose. Peña had resumed his seat and watched a parade of witnesses through half-glasses, showing increasingly less interest as the morning wore on. He passed a note to his neighbor, smiling like a schoolboy, and lit a cigarette, oblivious of the no-smoking sign posted on the wall just a few feet behind him. This face, that of the bored legislator who knew where the real deals were made, seemed more authentic than the teary penitent.

Still, the speech had served its purpose. The old woman who'd pronounced him shameless was definitely in the minority. His East LA constituents had lined up to shake his hand, delaying the resumption of business for nearly an hour.

As I sat and watched him, I wondered whether he would have met with such unquestioning forgiveness had he been a white politician. Minority politicians liked to complain about being held to higher standards than their white counterparts by the press, but within their communities, even the most outrageous behavior was often pardoned. I understood the reasons for this: mistrust of the media by people who were usually neglected by it and a hunger for leaders among groups who had for so long been without them. Still, when I analyzed what Peña had actually said in his defense, it amounted to a self-serving statement about the burdens of high office. He hadn't mentioned the fact that he had taken another man's life, much less expressed any remorse for it. His grief seemed directed at the setback to his career. I could have forgiven him for his human frailty but not his arrogance. By the time I heard my name called to testify I was incensed.

"Senators, ladies and gentlemen," I began, "I don't think anyone disagrees that there is a growing problem with gang violence in the poorest neighborhoods of the city. This bill, however, will not solve that problem. It will make it worse. This bill is a blank check for the police to come in and round up young men and women because of how they dress, or who they choose as their friends, or simply because the police don't like their looks."

"Excuse me," Peña cut in. "You are a criminal defense lawyer, aren't you, Mr. Rios."

"That's right, Senator."

"And isn't it true that you have defended gang members in the past?"

"What is that supposed to mean?"

He lurched forward, startled by my asperity. "Well, Mr. Rios, I don't think anyone's surprised about what side you're taking."

"I defend criminals, Senator, but I'm not one myself. Can you make the same statement?"

Everything got very quiet. Peña nodded slowly, as if he'd taken my measure, but I could see he was struggling for a response that wouldn't make him appear completely hypocritical.

"I guess I'm going to have to get used to that kind of smear," he said.

"You have a homicide charge hanging over your head, Senator. That's not a smear, it's a statement of fact."

"My personal problems don't have anything to do with this hearing," he replied.

"Nor does the fact that I'm a defense lawyer," I snapped back. "So if you'll stop imputing my character, I won't discuss yours."

With a dismissive shrug, he leaned back into his chair and focused his attention on the ceiling. I finished my statement and left the podium, catching sight of Tomas Ochoa who winked approval. Ignoring him, I headed for the door. I heard someone at my back running toward me. I stopped and turned. It was Peña's aide. Breathlessly he said, "Senator Peña would like to talk to you for a minute."

"About what?"

"I don't know, but he's waiting."

Curious, I followed the aide back up the aisle and through a door that led to a small anteroom behind the chamber. Peña was slouching against the wall, smoking. When he saw me, he dropped the cigarette, crushed it, and extended his hand with a broad grin.

"Henry," he said. "It's nice to see you again." My expression must have been as blank as my mind at that moment because he added helpfully, "Last year at the MALDEF dinner. You were with Inez Montoya."

"Of course," I said, remembering that he had been glad-handing at Councilwoman Montoya's table.

He wagged a genial finger at me. "You were pretty tough on me out there."

"You deserved it," I replied.

He clamped his hand on my shoulder, massaging it with thick fingers. "It's all a show, Rios. Nothing personal."

"Under the circumstances, Senator, that's a remarkably cynical thing for you to say."

He dug his fingers deeper into my shoulder. "Henry, truce, OK?"

"Sure," I said.

"Listen, we'll let the courts decide whether my bill is constitutional. That's not what I wanted to talk to you about."

"No?"

He dropped his hand from my shoulder, lit another cigarette, and with a curt nod dismissed his aide. "I fucked up good in Sacramento, Rios. I killed a man, and I hurt a lot of other people." His long face took on a distant, pained expression. "I'm still hurting a lot of people. I read that piece about you in the *Times*, he continued. "You've been where I am."

He referred to a profile that had appeared in the paper a few months earlier which appeared under the caption "Gay crusader fights for the underdog." The reporter had been thorough in his research, even prevailing upon my sister to describe our bleak childhood, not to mention my own stays at alcohol rehabs over the years, and the fact that my lover was HIV-positive. He seemed to regard these matters as evidence of my saintliness. Reading his piece had made me want to change my name and move to another state.

I said, "The reporter was looking for a hero."

"I'm looking for a friend," Peña said. "Someone who knows what it feels like to fail a lot of people who look up to him."

"I know what it feels like to fail myself," I replied.

"Yeah, well," he exhaled a plume of smoke, "that's the most humiliating part, isn't it? I made myself into somebody from nothing, Rios, just like you. Sure, I made mistakes along the way, but there wasn't anyone to tell me how to do it right. But I got most of it right, anyway," he said, tapping his chest. "Only this thing that happened up there, I don't understand it."

"What don't you understand, Gus?"

"How I got so out of control. I mean, the one thing I know about is control."

"Control's an illusion, Gus," I said. "Being born is like being tossed from a cliff. Grabbing on to the rocks that are falling around you doesn't keep you from falling. You just fall faster."

He smiled bleakly. "What's the difference if you still hit the ground?"

"You can always learn to fly."

He put his cigarette out on the marble wall behind us. "Is that what you do?"

"I'm still letting go of the rocks myself."

"You're a good man, Rios. Can I give you a call sometime?"

"Of course." I gave him a business card, pausing to write my home number on it.

He examined the card, slipped it into his wallet, and patted me on the back. "Say a prayer for me."

I watched him slip back into the council chamber, ashamed of the way I had taken him on during the hearing, but not entirely convinced that I hadn't just been brilliantly manipulated.

CHAPTER

TWO

▼

It was nearly noon when I left City Hall. I found a phone, checked in with my secretary, Emma Austen, and returned calls. When I finished, I still had an hour before a court appearance at the Criminal Courts Building, just across the street from City Hall, so I called home to invite Josh to come and eat lunch with me. All I got was his voice on our answering machine, urging me to leave a message. I hung up.

There had been a time when the course of his day was as familiar to me as mine. Now, I stood there for a moment, wondering where he might be. It was spring break at UCLA, so I knew he wasn't in class, but beyond that, I could only guess. I began walking to a sandwich shop in the Civic Center mall. It was warm and smoggy. The only sign of spring was the flowering jacarandas, bleeding purple blossoms onto the grimy sidewalks.

On the way to the sandwich shop, I passed a bookstore. Displayed in the windows was a book entitled *Vows: How to Make Your Marriage Work*. I stopped and read the book jacket, which promised new solutions to old marital problems. What about when one of you has a terminal disease and the other doesn't? Each time Josh's T-cell count dropped, I felt him drift further away from me, into his circle of Act Up friends, and his seropositive support group. Josh had become an AIDS guerrilla, impatient with my caution. Just that morning, bickering again over the wisdom of outing closeted gay politicians, he'd snapped, "Spoken like a true neggie," as if being negative for the virus was a defect of character.

Our arguments were no longer intellectual disagreements. He had adopted an "us vs. them" mentality over AIDS, and the more anxious he felt about his own health, the more strident he became. There might have been less ferocity in our quarrels had we been able to talk about his anxiety, as we once had, but he had decided that even this, or perhaps especially this, was beyond my understanding. I reacted with my own anger at being treated like an enemy by the man with whom I'd shared the last five years of my life.

I went into the bookstore and bought the book, suffering the sales clerk's sympathetic glance as he stuffed it into a bag. Over a limp ham sandwich I flipped through the chapters. Finding nothing relevant, I buried it in my briefcase and set off to court, the one place where I knew the rules.

I arrived in court a few minutes late. The deputy district attorney, an amiable man named Kelly Miller, who had been chatting with the clerk, said to me, "Your kid's a no-show, Henry."

'My kid' was a twenty-two-year-old gay man named Jimmy Dee, Deeds on the street, where his deeds were legion. He was a beautiful black boy with a luminous smile, undeniable charm, a four-page rap sheet for hustling and theft, and a romantic attachment to heroin. His last boyfriend, a much older man, had had him arrested for stealing from him to support his habit. After grueling negotiations, I had persuaded the boyfriend, Miller, and the judge to let Deeds plead to trespass on condition that he enter a drug rehab. The purpose of this hearing was for him to submit proof that he'd found a bed somewhere. He was being given a break, a fact that I impressed upon him at every opportunity. When I did, he would turn his kleig light smile on me and say, "I know, Mr. Rios, I know. God put you in my life."

"He's not that late," I said.

"Fifteen minutes late." Judge Patricia Ryan strode out of her chambers, arranging the bow of her blouse over her judicial robe. She was a patrician black woman with an acute street sense. "I don't know why I let you talk me into this, Henry. I should have had your client led away in manacles."

Although she was joking, I could tell she was irate.

"The case would have fallen apart without this deal," I said. "The boyfriend is deeply in the closet. He wouldn't have testified."

Miller said, "Your kid copped out, Henry. I could've convicted him on his statement."

"Juries aren't buying cop-outs from black defendants in LA these days," I replied.

Judge Ryan said, "Save this, gentlemen. I'm going to issue an arrest warrant."

"Wait, Judge, will you hold it one day? I'll go out looking for him."

She narrowed her eyes. "We've given him every opportunity."

"Let's give him one more."

"Mr. Miller?" she asked.

Kelly shrugged, "Why not? I'm sure Henry's not getting paid for this extra work."

She took her seat on the bench. "OK. *People versus Deeds*. The defendant is not in court. I will issue an arrest warrant to be held until tomorrow morning. Good luck, Mr. Rios."

"Thank you, Your Honor."

I called Josh from a phone in the corridor and found him at home. I explained that I was going in search of Deeds and might not be in until late.

"I won't be here anyway. There's an Act Up demo at

Antonovich's house," he said, referring to a particularly reactionary county supervisor.

"This is the first I've heard of it."

"I can't tell you everything."

That solved the mystery of where he had been when I'd called earlier.

"Is this a lawful demonstration, or am I going to be bailing you out of jail?"

Coolly, he replied, "The worst that ever happens is that they hold us overnight."

"I'd rather you didn't get arrested."

"Worried about your image?"

"I'm worried about your health."

He sniped, "That's not your problem."

I took a deep breath. "In that case, Josh, do whatever you want."

"I will," he said, and clanged the receiver down.

I hung up and immediately called back, but the line was busy, and stayed busy until I finally gave up.

Eight hours later, I found myself in the company of my investigator, Freeman Vidor, pulling into the parking lot of the Santa Monica Motel in West Hollywood. It was a perfunctory, two-floor stucco building wedged on a small lot just off the boulevard within walking distance of the gay bars; the kind of place where the vacancy sign was perennially lit.

"Is this it?" Freeman asked.

"Yeah, his last known address."

We got out of the car and went into the dimly lit office. An Asian woman stood behind the desk watching us apprehensively.

"Yes," she said.

Freeman produced a mug shot of Deeds and his private investigator's license. "We're looking for this kid."

"Police?" she inquired, holding up his license to the light.

"I'm a private cop," he said. "This is Mr. Rios, the kid's lawyer."

She took stock of me in my sincere blue suit, trying to puzzle it out.

"We're not here to make any trouble," I told her. "The boy calls himself Deeds. He has to be in court tomorrow morning."

We all stood there for a moment while she weighed her options. An air conditioner hummed loudly. Although glossy brochures advertised Gray Line tours and fun at Disneyland from a metal rack on a table in the corner, I doubted whether this place attracted that kind of trade.

"Twenty-three," she said, wearily. "Don't kick in the door."

Deeds's room was upstairs. I knocked a couple of times, then called him. I tried the door. Locked.

"We'll have to ask her to let us in," I said.

"Go admire the view," Freeman said.

I walked over to the railing and watched the traffic stream up and down the boulevard. A blond in a Jeep cruised by slowly, his cassette player blaring a disco tune from the seventies. Ah, the hunt, I thought, remembering the nights I had stood in San Francisco bars listening to that same song while I ingested a little liquid courage. Or, rather, a lot of liquid courage. Most nights I would stagger out alone and take the train back to school. Once in a while someone would pick me up, or I would pick him up, and I would toil in a stranger's bed for a few hours, trying to get out of my skin by going through his. I imagined that I was having fun, and sometimes I was, but not nearly often enough.

By the time I had graduated from law school, I was doing my drinking at home. That went on for a decade or so, drinking and working. By the time I sobered up, I was casting a pretty thin shadow, there being not much more to me than a vague alcoholic melancholy and the ability to work sixteen-hour days. I didn't work that hard anymore, and when I was unhappy, there was usually a reason. I was unhappy now, watching the blond cruise by, wondering with whom Josh was having an affair. The thought had been in the back of my mind for months but only now, as I stood in the sexy airs of Boystown, did it all fall into place: the element of evasion in his behavior which had never been there before, the vagueness about where he was going, and when he would be coming back. I hadn't lost track of him; he was hiding from me.

"Henry."

I glanced back at Freeman. He was holding the door open.

We stepped inside to a darkened room. "Deeds," I called. A sliver of light seeped out from beneath a door at the other end of the room. I went over and knocked. "Jimmy, are you in there?"

When there was no answer, I turned the knob and shoved the door open.

"Oh, shit," Freeman muttered.

Naked, Jimmy Dee sat sloppily on the toilet, his head tilted back at an angle that would have been really painful had he been alive. A needle was still jammed into his arm. His mouth was open and he stared up at a water stain on the ceiling in the shape of Africa.

I closed the door and said to Freeman, "Go downstairs and call 911."

After he left, I switched on the light and looked around the room. Deeds's clothes were in a pile at the foot of the unmade bed. There was a twenty on the nightstand, wages for his last trick, no doubt. On the dresser was a little pile of papers. I examined them and found my card, some phone numbers and an envelope addressed to Judge Ryan with the return address of SafeHouse, the same rehab that Gus Peña had been in. I tucked the envelope into my pocket.

Josh had left the kitchen window open and the room smelled faintly of the anise that grew wild down the side of the hill from our house. He wasn't there. I poured myself a glass of water and sat down at the kitchen table with the envelope I'd taken from Deeds's room. Inside was a letter from Edith Rosen, M.F.C.C., attesting to the fact that Deeds was scheduled to enter SafeHouse the following Monday, three days hence.

"You little shit," I said aloud, but what I felt was more grief than

anger. In my work, I was used to losing, but I thought I'd staked out
a tiny victory with Deeds.

But then, I'd always had a weakness for junkies, for their
defeated, helpless charm. Of course I knew better. My own fight
with the bottle had taught me intimately everything there was to
know about addiction. Drunks and junkies all had a big hole in
their gut that sucked in panic like Pandora's box in reverse unless
it was already filled by booze or a fix. Eventually, that stopped
working, and the panic went out of control until the only thing left
was dying. Sometimes, like Deeds, death is what you got and sometimes, like me, you were given a reprieve, but there was no logic
about it. Even if you lived, the panic was still there. It only faded
when you began see it for what it was, the long drop from darkness
to darkness, and you stopped fighting.

At that moment I could feel the panic elbowing me, tossing up
the image of Deeds in that grisly motel bathroom, reminding me of
every grisly room through which I had stumbled drunk, so close to
dying myself. And when that didn't get me going, the panic asked,
"Where's Josh?" a sure-fire tactic. I got up from the kitchen table
and went into the bedroom, switching on the lamp and stretching
out on the bed, still unmade from that morning. A book was half-
buried in the covers, the paperback edition of *Borrowed Time,* Paul
Monette's moving tale of his lover's death of AIDS. Josh had been
reading it.

It was after eleven. The demonstration was certainly over by now.

I sat up and fumbled for the TV remote control, flicking on the
set at the foot of the bed. I switched channels until I found some
local news, looking for a report about the Act Up demonstration.
Instead, I found myself watching Agustin Peña, standing against
the backdrop of the city council chamber, his arm draped around
his son who gazed at his father with a look that conveyed a history
of betrayal. Peña was saying, "My kids have always made me
proud, now I want them to be able to say the same thing about me."
Little Peña didn't seem to be buying it.

Watching them, I thought of my father, and about pride and

about betrayal. I shut off the TV, got undressed and into bed, ready for a long night.

"How was the demonstration?" I asked the next morning, pouring myself a cup of coffee as I waited for my bagel to toast. I had been asleep when Josh had come in. Waking beside him, my face against his bare back, I had breathed another man's smell on his body.

Shaggy-haired and heavy-lidded, he sat at the kitchen table in boxers, mixing an assortment of liquid vitamins into his organic cranberry juice.

He looked up at me. "It was great, Henry. The cops were wearing thick plastic gloves and riot helmets. You could tell they were terrified that one of us might bite them."

"Anyone get arrested?"

He finished mixing his holistic cocktail. "No, the cops told us that Antonovich wasn't even in town, so after an hour we split."

The toaster oven clicked and I retrieved my bagel. Buttering it, I asked, as casually as I could manage, "What did you do then?"

"Drove Steven home," he said, straining for equal nonchalance. "Sat and talked to him for awhile. Did you find your client?"

I sat down at the table. "Yes, as a matter of fact. In a motel room in Boystown. He was dead."

"Murdered?" he asked, putting his drink down.

"He OD'd."

"I'm sorry, Henry. I know how much you liked that kid."

I crunched into the bagel. "Not as much as I like you, Josh."

I watched him take a slug of juice, watched the muscles in his neck contract as he weighed a response. "What do you mean, Henry?"

"Who is he, Josh? Who are you sleeping with?"

"Steven," he said, immediately.

I thought back. Our house had become a kind of activists' club-house and frequently I came home to find a meeting raging in the living room. Though Josh had introduced me to many of the men and women who attended these sessions, their faces blurred in my mind into a single youthful face flushed with excitement and anger.

Steven?

Then I saw him. A little taller than Josh, about my height, muscular, good-looking. Not one of the big talkers, but the others listened when he did speak. Josh had mentioned once that Steven was one of the oldest surviving PWAs in the group, having been diagnosed eight years earlier.

Josh was speaking, "I kept meaning to tell you, but it seems like we never see each other anymore . . . "

"Are you saying this happened because I've neglected you?"

"No," he said. "It happened because I'm in love with him."

"Are you sure it's not because you're in love with his diagnosis?"

He stared at me in disbelief, and then fury.

"I'm sorry, Josh, I didn't mean that."

"You meant it all right," he said, pushing his chair back from the table. He stalked out of the house. I heard his car start up. I didn't think he would be coming back soon.

▲

CHAPTER

THREE

▼

I LEFT JOSH A LONG, APOLOGETIC NOTE AND SET OFF TO WORK. DRIVING in, I decided to stop at SafeHouse, to inform Edith Rosen, M.F.C.C., that Jimmy Dee would not be needing a bed there after all. I also thought I might say hello to Chuck Sweeny, the founder and director of the house, with whom I'd served on the local alcoholism council. After my term expired, he had urged me to keep in touch, but I had never followed up on my vague promises to drop in. Halfway there, it occurred to me that my true reason for going was that I felt like a creep for what I'd said to Josh and I was looking for a good deed to do by way of expiation.

SafeHouse sat at the bottom of one of the canyons in old Hollywood on a busy street lined with towering palm trees. Up in the canyon itself, the one-time movie star residences had been torn down over the years by the new rich who preferred less ostentatious aeries, but down where Cahill Court flattened out the buildings retained their old magnificence: rambling Italian villas and Normandy chateaux set back from the road by walls and fences and sweeping swaths of grass.

SafeHouse had been the mansion of a forties star who drank away his career. A few years before he died, he was led to sobriety by Chuck Sweeny, self-proclaimed recovering wino whom the actor had met when he stumbled into an AA meeting in skid row. In gratitude, the actor left Chuck his enormous residence which he stipulated in his will was to be used as an alcoholism recovery house.

The neighbors were horrified, but Sweeny persisted, fighting zoning boards and obdurate bureaucrats until SafeHouse became a reality. The neighbors still complained. Fortunately for Chuck, the drugged-out sixties arrived. In a bold move, Chuck announced that he would also take drug addicts into the house. For this, he was condemned by old-line AA-types for whom alcohol and drugs were two entirely separate universes. But Chuck's prescience paid off handsomely. As the decade progressed, the children of his affluent neighbors increasingly turned on, tuned in, and dropped out, and they found themselves in need of his services. His work with the rich and famous made SafeHouse chic long before Betty Ford took her last drink.

Strictly speaking, SafeHouse was a halfway house rather than a drying out sanatorium. Its residents signed up for a three-month program, the purpose of which was to integrate them back into society. There was no medical staff, just lay counselors, many of them former residents themselves. From what I knew about the place, talking to Chuck and to people who had been through it, sobriety was enforced by a set of rules that covered every aspect of the residents' lives, constant group meetings, and periodic drug and alcohol testing.

All of this was consistent with its motto, "A tough place for tough people," and reflected the personality of its founder. Chuck Sweeny was manipulative, inflexible, egotistical and extremely effective.

* * *

A high brick wall surrounded the front of the house. I parked on the street and walked up the driveway. The house was a three-story circus of a building, all gables, dormers, chimneys, conical roofed towers, bay windows, and a wraparound veranda supported by Corinthian columns; one expected to catch a glimpse of Morticia Addams at an upstairs window. A young man was mowing the lawn, his thin arms streaked with track marks. The sign on the door said, "You are home."

Inside, in the foyer, a young black woman sat at a desk reading the big book of Alcoholics Anonymous. She peered up at me and said, in practiced cadences, "Welcome to SafeHouse, sir. May I help you?"

"I'd like to see Edith Rosen," I replied.

She glanced down at a log. "Ms. Rosen's not in yet. Would you care to wait?" She smiled haplessly, clearly a resident practicing at being an ordinary human being. I knew the feeling.

"Is Chuck around?"

"Yes, sir, Chuck's here, but you need an appointment."

I handed her a business card. "Maybe he'll see me for a minute if you tell him who I am."

She read the card and picked up the phone, dialing an extension. "There's a Mr. Henry Rios here who would like to see you." She smiled at me, nervously. "Oh, OK, I'll send him in." She hung up. "Just go straight back down the hall, past the dining room and you'll see his office."

"Thank you," I said. "You've been very helpful."

"Thank *you*," she replied cheerily.

Straight down the hall proved to be a considerable distance. The house's rococo facade was belied by the shabbiness of its furnishings. The walls were all painted the same yellowing shade of cream and posted on them were long hand-written lists of the house's rules, along with inspirational messages along the lines of "One

Day At A Time," and "Don't Leave Five Minutes Before the Mira-cle," in Gothic script on parchment paper. The place reeked of stale cigarette smoke. Its many rooms all seemed to be occupied by people urgently, if mysteriously, engaged. In the dining room a mid-dle-aged man looked up from the table he was polishing and gazed at me blankly. A girl sat in a phone booth whispering and giggling into the phone. From behind a closed door came shouting and then weeping.

I pushed open a door marked "Administration" and stepped into a big room where several people sat at desks, hovered around file cabinets or fielded calls. Past them was an open door through which I saw Chuck Sweeny sitting at a beat-up desk, reading.

"Hi, Chuck," I said.

He looked up from his reading, and peered at me over the top of his glasses. A shock of gray hair swept over a red, drinker's face. Long thin arms stained with age poked out of rolled-up shirt sleeves. His shirt was unbuttoned and a thatch of white chest hair spilled over a yellowed T-shirt. Chuck looked the part of someone who had once slept in the streets of every skid row from Seattle to San Diego.

"Henry R.," he said, quickly demoting me from lawyer to fellow drunk. "Come in, come in, come in."

I sat down. "This is quite a place you've got here."

"This your first time?" he asked incredulously. I thought guiltily of my promise to have visited sooner.

"I'm afraid so."

"Never as a resident?" he asked, his eyes twinkling.

"Not yet."

"Well let's hope you never are," he said. "So, do you want the tour?"

"Actually, I'm here on business. One of my clients was supposed to check in on Monday, but he's not going to make it. He overdosed last night."

"Too bad," he said briskly. "Too bad."

"He was carrying a letter from Edith Rosen."

"Oh, Edie. Did you talk to her already?"

"I was told she wasn't in. She's a professional isn't she, an M.F.C.C.?"

"Marriage, Family and Child Counselor," he replied sardonically. "Don't that cover all the bases."

"I didn't think you used professionals here."

"Times change, we change with 'em."

"Well, anyway, my client's name was James Dee."

He jotted a note. "Listen Henry, as long as you're here, I wonder if I could run a little something by you, law-wise."

"Sure," I said. "Is the house having a legal problem?"

"Close the door, would you?"

I reached back and pulled the door shut.

"Maybe," he said. "Maybe. That's what I'm hoping you could tell me. This is the situation. You see, one of our residents, hotheaded little guy, well he's a patient of Edie's, and it seems he told her that he was going to kill another resident, ex-resident now; he checked out last week." He jerked his head toward me. "You following?"

"Perfectly."

"Good, good. So this little guy makes this threat and I find out about it."

"From the therapist?"

"I hear about it," he continued, "and, of course, I'm concerned, a mite concerned, anyway. I mean, shit, Henry, people are always threatening to kill each other around here, but this guy, well, he don't seem to want what we have to offer."

"What exactly do you want to do? Expel the kid?"

"Well, now that's where you come in, Henry. See, I want to throw him out, but you know, there's paperwork," he shuffled through a stack of files on his desk. "Seems I have to document my reasons," he said caustically. "For the state, because they give us money now. But Edie says she can't say anything about what the kid told her because there's some privilege these days between patients and counselors, like the kind you have with priests or," he twinkled at me, "lawyers. But that can't be right, can it? I mean, he threatened to kill this guy."

"There is a psychotherapist-patient privilege," I said, "but it's not absolute. In some cases a therapist does have a duty to warn a third party if one of the therapist's clients has made a threat against that person. Otherwise, the therapist could be sued if anything actually happened."

"Exactly," Chuck said, shedding his vague, folksy manner. "That's *exactly* what I told her, and I told her that that means the house could be on the line. But damned if she refuses to cooperate. Maybe if she heard it from you."

"Chuck, the privilege also doesn't apply if someone other than the patient and the therapist know about the threat. You know. Why don't you expel the kid?"

"I need Edie to back me up," he said grimly. "Let's go find her. It'll just take a minute of your time."

We found her in a large closet beneath the stairwell that evidently served as her office. A small metal desk was shoved across the space and against the wall, leaving enough room behind the desk for her chair and a file cabinet. Her phone was connected to a jack outside the room by a long, tangled cord. An uncovered light bulb hung down from the ceiling providing the room's only light. The trod of footsteps on the stairs was audible above us. The only other furniture was another chair wedged between the back wall and her desk. Anyone sitting on it would have to have sat spread-legged. On the corner of her desk was a vase that held a white rose.

"Edie," Chuck said, "there's someone I'd like you to meet, an old friend of mine, Henry Rios, the lawyer. You probably heard of him."

Edith Rosen was a short, stocky woman in her early fifties, it looked like. Her plain face was comfortably lived-in but her gray eyes were wary and when she spoke there was an edge to her voice.

"I'm sorry, I haven't heard of Mr. Rios. Is there a problem?"

I decided it would be a good idea to disassociate myself from Chuck whom apparently she disliked. "I stopped by to let you know that Jimmy Dee overdosed last night."

I handed her the letter she had written for Deeds. She looked at it and then at me, "Deeds?"

"I found it in his room. He didn't show up in court yesterday, so I went out looking for him."

"Ah," she said, blinking. "Poor Deeds. He was your client?"

"Yes."

"I'm so sorry." She turned the envelope over and said, softly, "Deeds."

"I appreciate the letter," I said.

She gave me a tired smile. "He told me, 'God must have put you in my life.'"

"Yes, he was fond of invoking God," I replied.

"Maybe God answered," Chuck said.

She put the envelope on her desk. "Maybe your God, Chuck," she replied, then said to me, "Chuck is one of those AA fundamentalists who thinks you're better off dead than still drinking or using."

I said, "I can't imagine any circumstances where anyone is better off dead."

My answer pleased her.

Chuck cleared his throat and said, "Henry wants to talk to you about something else, too, Edie. That situation we discussed yesterday."

I quickly said, "Well, actually Chuck, you asked me about it."

"I know, I know, and thank you for taking it on. You two talk, all right? I'll be in my office." He scurried out of the room, leaving me to face a clearly irritated Rosen.

"May I sit down?" I asked.

"Sit."

I arranged myself uncomfortably in the chair and said, "This wasn't my idea, Edith."

"What did he tell you?" she demanded.

"He told me that one of your patients threatened the life of another patient, and that he wanted to expel him, but he needed you to back him up, and you refused."

"Did he tell you why?" she asked in the same, unyielding tone.

"The psychotherapist privilege."

"No," she said, "I mean, did he tell you why he needs me to back him up?"

"No."

"Because he found out about it by rummaging through my files when I wasn't here."

"I see," I said. "I wondered why he just didn't go ahead and expel the guy since it seemed that the privilege had been waived."

"The privilege is waived by disclosure," she said, "not by breaking into the therapist's files."

"Why would Chuck do something like that?"

"Look around you, Mr. Rios," she said, her eyes sweeping the tiny room. "It's no accident that I'm in here. The Board of Directors forced Chuck to hire me because the state required it for Safe-House to keep its funding, but he has no use for me. As far as Chuck is concerned, all you need to get sober is the big book and a few AA meetings."

"It's worked for a lot of people," I observed.

"It doesn't work for everyone," she fired back. "The relapse rate for people coming into AA is ninety percent. Those nine out of ten obviously need something more."

"How does this explain why Chuck rifled your files?"

"He thinks I'm a subversive," she said. "He wants to know what I'm telling the residents."

"Look," I said, "putting all that aside for a moment, this situation that he described does involve potential liability for you and the house if your patient carried out his threat."

"I know the law in this area, Mr. Rios, every therapist does. If I seriously thought that Michael was a threat to Gus ..." She stopped abruptly, and took a sharp breath. "You didn't know their names, did you?"

I shook my head.

"Sometimes when I'm angry I blurt things out that I shouldn't," she said, smiling wanly. "Freudian slip."

"As long as the cat's out of the bag," I replied, "do you mean Gus Peña?"

"You know him?"

"I was at City Hall yesterday when he gave his little speech," I said, "and I talked to him afterwards."

Sternly, she said, "My mentioning their names was completely inadvertent."

"I'm not going to warn him," I said. "I do think you should, however."

"What I was going to say," she continued, "is that it's my professional judgment that the threat was not serious. Look, there was tremendous conflict between Michael and Gus while Gus was here. Obviously, I can't go into the details, but I'm satisfied that Michael was simply expressing some anger. He's not about to kill Gus Peña."

"All right," I said, "but what are you going to do about Chuck?"

"I'll handle Chuck," she said.

I untangled myself from the chair. "I appreciate what you tried to do for Deeds." I gave her a business card. "If you decide you need my help over this situation, call me. Chuck doesn't have to be involved."

She took the card. "Thank you, Mr. Rios."

"Henry," I said. I stood at the doorway, looking at her. Despite her occasional asperity, Edith Rosen struck me as a very trustworthy person. I was tempted to talk to her about my troubles with Josh. Instead, I asked, "If I were going to see a therapist, and I wanted to see someone like you, who would you recommend?"

"Someone like me?" she asked, smiling. "You mean a specialist in recovery?"

"No, I mean, someone I wouldn't mind telling my secrets to."

"What are your secrets, Henry?" she asked kindly.

"I live with a man who has AIDS," I said, "and I think I need to talk to someone about it."

She nodded thoughtfully. After a moment, she said, "Why don't you call Raymond Reynolds. I think he has a lot of experience counseling gay men. Here, I'll give you his number." She flipped through a Rolodex, and jotted a name and number on a piece of paper.

"Thanks," I said.

It was still early when I got to the office, and Emma hadn't yet arrived. I put on the coffee, checked the mail and went into my office. Josh was sitting on the couch, looking out the window. He looked worn out. There was an ashtray with three butts in it beside him. He hadn't smoked in a couple of years. I sat down.

"Hello," I said.

He looked at me unsmilingly and said, "Hi."

"I'm really sorry about what I said this morning."

"I'm sorry about what you said this morning, too," he replied. "And I'm . . . ," he hesitated. "Well, I'm sorry I ran out on you. I should've stayed." He lit a cigarette.

"When did you start that again?"

He exhaled. "Ten minutes after I left the house."

It was really bad if he was smoking again. "Are you leaving me, Josh?"

"Don't I get to give my speech?" he asked, smiling briefly. "I've been sitting here practicing."

"I'm listening."

He stubbed out the cigarette. His long fingers trembled and I hurt for him. "We've had a lot of fights, lately, Henry, but you've never said anything as vicious as what you said about Steve. Maybe I drove you to it. I mean, I have been lying to you, whether you knew it or not."

"I knew."

He touched my hand. "Please let me finish without a fight."

"OK, sorry."

"The other thing I realized is that you're right, half-right, anyway. I'm not in love with Steve's diagnosis, but I am in love with his courage, the same way I was in love with your courage when I first met you. Do you remember how I was? I was a closet case who knew that being HIV-positive was the judgment of God for letting myself get fucked in the ass." He grimaced. "You taught me I could be gay and still live with dignity. You taught me to be brave."

"It works both ways, Joshua."

"I'd like to think so, Henry," he said, the sentence drifting off. "I need something else now."

"Josh, I can change."

His eyes filled with tears. "This isn't easy for me."

"Give me a chance," I said. "Look, if the problem is me, let me try to do something about it. I'll see a therapist."

"The problem isn't you," he said. "The problem is that I'm dying."

"You're not dying, Josh."

He wiped his face on his sleeve. "Just because I'm not sick right now doesn't mean I'm all right."

"You are all right."

He sighed. "Go see your therapist, Henry. It can't hurt, but I need some time to myself. I'm going to be staying with my parents for awhile."

"All right," I said, "as long as it doesn't mean you're going for good. It doesn't, does it?"

He shook his head. "We'll talk. I want to go home, now, and get some things." He stood up, and lay his hand on my face. "I wish this wasn't happening."

"Nothing's happened, yet," I said.

After he left, I sat at my desk and everything that I'd kept at bay while we were talking washed over me, wave after wave of memory, grief, regret, while I told myself it wasn't over yet. When I trusted myself to talk, I called Raymond Reynolds.

▲

CHAPTER

FOUR

▼

THE HOUSE WAS DARK WHEN I GOT HOME THAT NIGHT. OUT OF HABIT, I switched on lights and opened windows as I made my way through the warm, stuffy rooms and at first glance nothing was different. It was only when I let myself notice that I saw a few small things were missing: the bottles of vitamins that lined the kitchen counter, a striped bathrobe, the paperback copy of *Borrowed Time*. In the bedroom, I got out of my suit and tie and tossed them on the bed instead of hanging them in the closet, and pulled on the sweatpants that had been left lying on the floor. I went back into the kitchen and glanced at the counters looking for a note without really expecting to find one, and didn't. I took leftover pasta out of the refrigerator, poured myself a glass of mineral water, and went into the dining room to eat.

In my worst fantasies I had imagined coming home from Josh's funeral to a house still filled with his belongings and having to dispose of them. It had never occurred to me that I would one day come home to find those things already gone. This was not the grief for which I had prepared. I finished eating and left the plates on the table, picked up the paper and looked for the nearest movie. I sat through it twice and when I came home fell asleep in the guest room just before dawn.

The phone rang. I hopped out of bed and grabbed the nearest extension.

"Josh?"

"Uh, Henry Rios?" The voice was female and unfamiliar.

"Yes, this is Henry Rios."

"It's Edith Rosen. We talked yesterday at SafeHouse."

"Hello, Edith," I said, switching to the voice I used with clients, friendly but brisk. "Is something wrong?"

"Chuck told Michael he has to leave SafeHouse," she replied.

"Why, because of the threat he made about Gus Peña?"

"Yes," she said.

I sat down at the kitchen table and rubbed the sleep from my eyes. "I thought you had to sign off on that."

"Well he did it without me," she said sharply. "I assume he thinks he can get away with it."

"This is really directed at you, isn't it?"

"Of course it is," she replied. "And unless he's stopped it completely undermines my function here. No one's going to want to talk to me if what they say can be used to expel them."

"What's the situation, exactly?"

"This morning he called Michael into his office, confronted him with what he had said about Gus, and told him he had until noon to clear out. Michael called me. I'm calling you. That's the situation."

I got up and quietly started taking things out for coffee. "Is threatening another resident legitimate grounds for expulsion?"

"He didn't threaten another resident," she replied heatedly.

"But is it?" I asked, lighting the flame beneath the coffee pot.

"Yes," she said grudgingly. "The point is, Michael never threatened Gus directly and Chuck would never have known about it if he hadn't gone through my files."

"I understand that," I told her. "I just wanted to know Chuck's position."

Edith said, "You offered to help me, Henry. Well, I need your help. We've got to get Chuck to back down."

"What about going to the Board of Directors?"

"They don't meet for another month, and by then this will be ancient history and no one will understand what the fuss is all about. Besides, if Michael's expelled he'll be in violation of his pro—," she caught herself.

"Probation?"

"Well, I suppose it would have come out anyway."

"What's he on probation for?"

"He tried to rob a convenience store with a toy gun," she said. "He was so high on drugs at the time that he didn't even make it out the front door before the police arrived."

"Hang on a second." I put the phone down and found a pad of paper and a pencil. "OK, I'm back. Was this his first arrest or has he been stealing to support his habit?"

"He doesn't need to steal," she said. "His parents have money. He was trying to impress his friends in one of the gangs. He's desperate to belong, but he's too much of a crackhead even for them. He thought they'd let him in if he pulled off a robbery."

"What's his last name?"

"Ruiz," she said. "Michael Ruiz. His parents worked their way out of the barrio, but were too busy to raise a kid so they dumped him with his grandmother, who still lives there. What they wouldn't give him of their time, they tried to make up in money."

"How old is he?"

"Eighteen. He was a juvenile when he was arrested."

"That explains the armed robbery charge," I said, jotting notes. "The DA always overcharges juvies, to get their attention. Did he do any time?"

"A few months at a youth camp, and then they sent him to us

with three years hanging over his head. You can see what'll happen if Chuck throws him out."

"How's Michael's record at SafeHouse otherwise?"

"He's coming along," she said evasively.

"Level with me, Edith."

"He has a lot of resistance, but I was making some progress."

"What I meant is, other than this incident, does Chuck have any other legitimate grounds to expel him."

"No," she said decisively.

"All right, you and Michael come to my office. Make it about an hour. I'll try to figure something out between now and then."

"Thank you, Henry."

I hung up. The coffee was boiling. With a start, I realized I hadn't thought about Josh once while I was talking to Edith Rosen.

Edith was waiting at the door to my office when I arrived. Nearby, a thin young man skulked against the wall. A cigarette burned between his fingers. His sallow face was topped with a crown of unruly black hair and a tiny blue tear was tattooed at the corner of his right eye. He glanced at me without expression. Edith introduced us.

"Come inside," I said, unlocking the door. We went back to my office and I sat them down while I started my second pot of coffee that morning.

When I returned to the room, Michael was sitting in a self-consciously languid position, one jeaned leg thrown over the arm of the chair. He was smoking a fresh cigarette. There was a blankness in his face that made me want to snap at him to sit up straight and put out the cigarette. When I took a closer look, I saw the nervousness in his eyes as they shifted back and forth between Edith and me, like a child awaiting punishment.

"Can I assume you know what this is all about?" I asked him.

"Sure," he drawled.

"Then tell me."

He started to mumble, and I told him to speak up. He glared at me, then said, "That asshole *gabacho* wants to violate my probation because I said something to her about Peña."

I looked at Edith. "Close enough. You understand that Ms. Rosen didn't tell Mr. Sweeny anything that you said to her during your counseling session?"

"Yeah, that's what she says," he said skeptically. "So how did he find out?"

"That's not important," Edith said quickly. "The point is, he got that information without talking to me."

I wondered to myself why she hadn't told him that Chuck had gone through her files, and made a mental note to ask her about it when we were alone. In the meantime, I would have to trust her judgment on it.

"When you talk to a therapist," I told Michael, "the law protects what you say to her. Generally speaking, the only person who can tell anyone what you've said during therapy is you." I watched him during my explanation, and he seemed to be following me. "Do you understand that?"

"Yeah, I understand."

"Sometimes, a patient will tell a therapist that he wants to hurt someone, and if the therapist believes that the threat is real, then she has a duty to warn that person. In this case, Edith . . . "

"I knew that, even though you don't like Gus Peña, you didn't really plan to hurt him," she said quickly. "So I didn't say anything to him."

He sneered. "I'd jump that chump in a minute."

I let it go. "What I plan to do is call Chuck Sweeny and tell him that unless he allows you to stay at SafeHouse, we'll bring an action against him to force him to take you back."

Edith looked alarmed. "If you put it that way, he'll tell you to go ahead."

"I know Chuck, too," I told her. "I think I can make a deal with him."

"A deal? What are you going to offer him?" she asked.

"That Michael's attitude will improve dramatically if he's allowed to stay."

"Fuck that shit," he mumbled.

I cast a cold look at him. "These are your choices, Michael. I make a deal with Chuck that allows you to return to SafeHouse today, or we try to do it through the courts and take the chance that your probation will be violated anyway. You're eighteen now. The Youth Authority can hold you until you're twenty-one or you could be certified as an adult and sent to state prison."

"I don't care," he said, sinking into the chair.

Edith said, "Call Chuck."

"I need for Michael to wait outside," I said.

"Is that necessary?" she asked.

"Yes. You stay."

Michael extricated himself from his chair and rolled out of the room with a gangbanger's gait. I watched him, wondering what Edith saw in him worth going to all this trouble for.

After he'd slammed the door shut, I said, "Why didn't you tell him Chuck had gone through your files?"

"Michael doesn't need another reason to defy Chuck."

"He thinks you told him. I could see it in his face."

"It'll be easier for him to re-establish trust with me than with Chuck."

"That boy doesn't look like he trusts anyone," I said. "The other thing I wanted to ask you is why you cut me off when I was about to tell him that you didn't take his threat against Gus Peña seriously."

"It was the way you were saying it," she said in exasperation. "It implied that he's not to be taken seriously at all."

"You really care about this kid, don't you?" I asked, leaning back into my chair. "Why is that?"

"I care about all my clients," she insisted. "Are you going to call Chuck?"

"What's the number there?" I asked, and dialed as she gave it to me. I switched on the speaker. A moment later, I had Chuck on the line. While Edith leaned forward, I said, "Chuck, it's Henry Rios. I have Edith Rosen here with me in my office, and one of your residents, Michael Ruiz."

"Morning, Henry," he replied gruffly. "What's this all about?"

"I think you know, Chuck. The question is, what are we going to do about it?"

"Do about what? That boy broke a house rule. He's got to go."

Edith scowled and started to speak, but I put up a silencing hand.

"Listen, Chuck," I said in my friendliest voice, "if you and I were at an AA meeting, and I said I wanted to kill some old bastard, wouldn't you respect my anonymity? You wouldn't go running off to tell the guy. Anonymity is all about keeping confidences."

"It's not the same thing," he said flatly. "She's not in the program. She's not one of us."

"Chuck, it says in the big book that we can seek help outside the program if it's necessary to maintain our sobriety. All that happened here is that Michael sought Edith's help to maintain his sobriety by expressing an honest feeling. How else is he going to get well?"

"The quality of that kid's sobriety leaves a lot to be desired," he growled.

"Everyone has to start somewhere, Chuck. Look, there's obviously a turf war going on between you and Edith." Across the desk, Edith flushed angrily. "That's something the two of you are going to have to fight out. All I'm asking is that you not do it on this kid's back. Whatever you think of Edith, Michael is one of us, Chuck. And I can guarantee that if you take him back, his attitude will improve."

"What's the stick, Henry?" he asked.

"I beg your pardon?"

"You showed me the carrot, what's the stick?"

I could tell by his tone that it was time to level with him. "The law doesn't share your disdain for psychotherapy," I said. "In fact, the law protects the therapist and her patients. When you looked at Michael's file, without his permission, you violated the law, Chuck, and that could be a real problem for you and the house."

"I can't believe you would turn on your own kind."

"It's like I said, Chuck, Michael is also my kind."

After a moment, he said, "We'll take him back this time, but I better see some improvement."

"I'm sure you will," I said.

When I'd hung up, Edith said, "That was very duplicitous of you."

"Which part?"

"The way you played on your AA connection to him."

"Where's the duplicity? I believed every word I said. And, anyway, the alternative would have been to confront him, which even you admitted doesn't work with Chuck."

She smiled. "And you were willing to put me on the same level as him."

"You weren't my client in this case," I said. "Michael was. Speaking of whom, we'd better go tell him the good news."

For the rest of the day, and into Sunday, I worked at my office, going home only to sleep and check for messages from Josh. I didn't hear from him until late Sunday night.

"Cullen died," he said without preliminaries.

"Cullen McArthur?" I asked. Cullen had sold us our house four years earlier. "I saw him two weeks ago. He looked fine."

"He died this morning," Josh replied, and I could hear the fatigue in his voice. "I've been in and out of hospital all weekend."

"That's why you didn't call," I said, as much to myself as him.

"I'm sorry, Henry, but now is the first chance I've had."

"Now is fine," I said. "I miss you, Josh."

After a moment, he said, "I miss you, too."

And after that, there didn't seem to be much more to say, but we talked anyway, short bursts of trivia alternating with long pauses. After twenty minutes, Josh said, "I'm really tired."

"All right. Can I see you soon?"

"Cullen's memorial is on Tuesday at the church on Fountain and Fairfax, at two. Meet me there, OK?"

"I will. Good night, Josh."

"Good night, Henry," he said. "I love you."

After he hung up, I found myself thinking about the tattoo at the corner of Michael Ruiz's eye, an old gang tattoo that was supposed to remind its wearer of the sadness of life.

▲

CHAPTER

FIVE

▼

On Monday morning at eight o'clock I presented myself at the office of Raymond Reynolds, on the second floor of a red brick building that featured a faux colonial facade, in the part of Beverly Hills that its natives refer to disdainfully as "the flats." Reynolds's office was done entirely in tones of gray, from floor to ceiling; it was like being in a brain cell. He himself was a plump man with a round, friendly face and a soft, thoughtful voice. We got through the preliminaries and he asked me the inevitable question, "So, why are you here?"

I was stumped. None of the answers my mind was busily articulating seemed adequate, and after a few uncomfortable moments, that's what I told him.

"Why do you think that is, Henry?"

"You know, this is a funny situation for me," I said. "Usually I'm asking the questions."

He smiled, but did not respond, his question pendant, awaiting an answer.

"I guess it's because every answer I think of seems to be starting in the middle instead of the beginning," I said.

"What's the immediate cause of your being here?" he asked. "Let's start with that."

His leather couch squeaked as I shifted my weight. "My lover has moved out."

"And you didn't want him to."

"No," I said. "I didn't want him to. He has AIDS and he doesn't think I understand anymore, and he's found someone who he thinks does. I think I understand."

He cocked his head slightly. "What is it you think you understand?"

"His fear of dying."

Reynolds nodded, then asked, "And how is it that you understand that, Henry?"

For the second time he stumped me. I looked around the gray room, avoiding his mild, almost bovine gaze. It was very quiet in this room. It was not quiet in my head.

"Have you faced death?" he asked.

"I came back," I said, after a moment. "I came back from the dead."

"Tell me about that."

"I used to drink," I said. "About seven years ago I stopped. I was working on a case, a murder. My client was a kid who had read too much Ayn Rand, basically, and decided he was above the rules. He tried to prove it by going out one night with a butcher knife to a park where homeless people lived, and he stabbed a man to death." I looked at Reynolds who continued to gaze at me impassively. "Anyway, I was at home one evening going over the police report. I had pictures of the dead man spread out on the table. I was on my way to being drunk, as I was every night around that time, and I happened to look at the victim's face. His eyes were open. Have you ever seen a dead person's eyes?"

"Yes," he said, softly. "I have."

I nodded. "Well, then you know, there nothing as dead as a dead man's eyes. So, I looked at that picture, and I began to shake because I had seen those eyes before, that morning looking into the mirror." The images began to flood my mind and I had to stop for a moment. "I was thirty-three years old, and my life was working and drinking, and it had been for a long time, since I'd left home for college. Somewhere along the line, I had died."

"What does that mean, Henry?" he inquired in his mild voice.

"The thing that makes us human, the recognition of being alive, I had lost that. I drowned it in bourbon and kept myself so busy with work that I hadn't even noticed until that moment."

"What happened?"

I laughed. "I had a few more drinks, to calm myself, and more or less passed out. When I came to the next morning, I was panicked. So I had a few more drinks, and a few more. For two days, I got drunk and passed out, came to, and got drunk. Finally, a friend, a policewoman, came over to check up on me because I'd missed some court appearances. She put me in the hospital, and I dried out. If she hadn't come I would've killed myself, probably."

Reynolds nodded. "Let's go back. Before you left home to go away to college, what was that like for you?"

"You people always end up wanting to talk about mommy and daddy," I said, intending a joke, but it was more hostile than funny.

No slouch, Reynolds said immediately, "Your parents seem to be a touchy subject."

"Sorry," I replied. "It's just that I think I'm a little too old to be blaming them for my problems."

"Was there alcoholism in your family?"

I smiled at him. "I can't compliment you on your acuity because that's almost a truism, isn't it; alcoholic son, alcoholic father."

"Your father was alcoholic."

"Touché," I replied. "Yes, my father was a violent drunk."

"Violent toward you?" he pressed.

"Yes," I replied, aware of the impatience that had entered my voice as we talked about my father.

"Were you violent when you drank?"

"Of course not."

He grinned like a lawyer who's cornered a witness on cross-examination. "Why 'of course'?"

"I'm not at all like my father," I said.

"In what ways are you different?"

"Well, I'm homosexual, for one, and I'm educated, and I'm not a violent man."

"Interesting," he mused after a moment. "The first distinction is one you have no control over, and the second is one that I imagine you worked very hard for."

"Are you saying they're connected?"

"I think very frequently gay boys compensate for their homosexuality by excelling at some talent they have."

"Compensate," I repeated. "That suggests a deficiency."

"Very few boys regard their homosexuality in any other light," he said. "Did you?"

"No," I said. "No, I didn't want to be queer, either."

"Did you ever come out to your father?"

I shook my head. "I had to wait until he was dead before I came out, or I wouldn't be sitting here now, paying you to talk about him."

"The third distinction you made between you and your father is that you're not a violent man. What about the violence you directed against yourself?"

"I don't understand," I said.

"You said that at some point during your drinking, you died. Who killed you?"

I leaned back into the uncomfortable couch, and said, appreciatively, "You'd have made a good lawyer."

* * *

Reynolds's question stayed with me through the day, as I dashed across town, from Santa Monica to Pasadena, and then to the Criminal Courts Building arguing a motion in one court, conducting a preliminary hearing in another, and working out a plea bargain in the third. A typical Monday, in other words. I whizzed through the warm, hazy day, catching fragments of the city; a glittering, deserted beach, a shopping center whose signs were all written in Korean, the spooky Belle Epoque grandeur of Pasadena's domed city hall. Who killed Henry Rios? reverberated like the title of a pulp mystery in the corner of my head that wasn't occupied by a hundred other matters. Of course, I was the guilty party, so the next question was, what would be my defense?

That night I went to an AA meeting and overheard someone say he knew he was recovering when his thoughts turned from suicide to homicide. Reynolds was right, there was a streak of violence in me, and I had become my own unintended victim. The man I really wanted to kill was the father whom I had had so much trouble talking to him about. As he had done in so many other ways, my father had cheated me by dying before I could dispatch him. On that comforting thought, I fell asleep.

The next day, I got caught up in a hearing and arrived twenty minutes late to the church on Fairfax where Cullen McArthur's memorial service was being held. I went up the worn stairs to the auditorium and found it full of men sitting on folding chairs that creaked noisily as the mourners fidgeted in the musty heat of the dim room. Panels of stained glass cast shards of color across the dirty wooden floor. The room smelled, not of sanctity, but of Eternity, Obsession and a dozen other cloying male scents. A long table at the back held bowls of fruit, platters of bagels and cream cheese, and two mammoth coffee urns gurgling softly. I couldn't find Josh in the crowd so I took the first empty chair.

Cullen was known as Mary Louise to his closest friends. He had sold us our house but we really came to know him later, I through AA and Josh through Act Up.

At the front of the room was a podium and on either side of it were floral wreaths on easels. In the center of each were photographs of Cullen. One showed him as a boy of six or seven, bristly-haired and freckled. The other had been taken when he was in his mid-thirties, probably, a glossy head shot of a rather ordinary-looking man lighted and airbrushed into centerfold pulchritude. My own image of him was as a man with thinning red hair, very pale skin, mouth set in a moue, eyes wide with hot dish. Just another faggot, funny and sweet, just another sissy whose only sin had been not to be ashamed of himself.

At the podium, Cullen's best friend was saying, "The last time I went to see him, he'd gone completely blind. So I sat down and held his hand and said, 'Honey, I'm so sorry.' And Cullen squeezed my hand and said, 'Girlfriend, you don't know the half of it. I never learned how to put lipstick on in the dark.'"

I was laughing and crying at the same time, and then I saw Josh. He was weeping on the shoulder of the man sitting next to him. Steven. Steven lifted Josh's face and kissed his forehead, like an old lover. I got up quietly and left the room.

I was on the sidewalk, heading to my car when I heard someone call, "Henry."

It was Timothy Taylor, my AA sponsor, tall and thin, a sprig of lilac drooping from the lapel of his white silk blazer, his graying blond hair swept back in dramatic planes from his narrow, inquisitive face.

"I thought I saw you skulking in," he said, "and I definitely saw you skulking out."

"Back to work," I answered, not wanting to talk to him.

He put his arm through mine. "Could you believe that Rita Hayworth shot of Mary Louise? All she needed were castanets. Josh talked to me earlier."

"Oh," I said.

"Is there something you'd like to tell me?"

"I've been dumped, Tim, that's all."

"Mm," he replied. "Must hurt."

"Of course it hurts."

"So what are you going to do about it? Run away, just like you did when you saw Josh with Steve?"

"Is that such an unusual reaction?"

We were at my car. "I thought you came here to remember Cullen."

"I'll call you, Tim."

"Don't wait until you've had a drink before you do it," he replied.

Back at my office, I pretended to work, reading the same page of a reporter's transcript over and over, while entertaining murderous thoughts toward Steven. I was relieved when the phone rang. Emma said, "Senator Peña's on the line. We're coming up in the world."

"Just put him through, OK?"

"Excuse me, Mr. Rios," she replied.

"Sorry, Emma, I—"

"Who's Emma?" Gus Peña asked, jovially. "Your girlfriend?"

"My secretary, Gus. Are you still in town? I thought the senate was in session."

"Right now I have more important things to think about," he said. "Like an arraignment."

I closed the reporter's transcript and pulled out a legal pad. "I take it this is a business call."

"Listen, Rios, I got a lawyer up in Sacramento who doesn't know his ass from a hole in the ground. I've been asking around and I hear you're good. Take my case, all right?"

People versus Peña, I wrote at the top of the pad. "What do you want to do about the case, Gus? From what I hear they got you cold."

"That'll be the day," he laughed. "First thing is, I want the trial moved down here, to LA. The papers up in Sacramento already got me convicted and serving time."

Change of venue, pre-trial publicity, I wrote. "Moving the trial doesn't change the evidence."

"You haven't even seen the evidence," he said impatiently.

"You were arrested at the scene, weren't you?"

"There were two of us in the car, Rios, me and one of my aides. We were driving back from dinner. I wasn't driving. He was."

I put down my pen. "I beg your pardon?"

"You heard me, I wasn't driving."

"You were arrested."

"Sure, I was arrested," he said, as if this was a minor detail. "But let me tell you how it happened. Frank was drunker than I was. He hit the guy and stopped in the middle of the street. When he saw what he had done, he got out of the car and started running. I couldn't leave the car where it was, so I got in to pull it over. That's when the cops came."

"Why didn't you explain this to the police?"

"Listen, Rios, I'm a Chicano from East Los Angeles. When I saw the cops, the old homeboy instincts kicked in, and I wasn't about to tell them squat."

"You've had weeks since then to bring this to their attention," I observed.

He didn't miss a beat. "I had to convince Frank to come forward and accept responsibility. Without him, the story doesn't hold up."

"That's true," I said.

"You sound like you don't believe me, Rios." There was an edge to his voice.

"It's just that less than a week ago you told me you had killed the man."

"Yeah," he said, after a moment. "Well, I was protecting Frank. He's my homeboy, you know. That's all."

"I'd have to talk to both of you," I said.

"Sure, no problem. How about tomorrow?"

I checked my schedule. I was starting a trial downtown. "No, not tomorrow. Thursday afternoon, around four."

"You got it," he said. "We'll be there."

I hung up and doodled on the sheet of paper in front of me. *People versus Peña*, a defense lawyer's dream; high-profile case, cooperative client, an ironclad defense. All in all, it sounded too good to be true.

▲

CHAPTER

SIX

▼

JOSH CALLED ME THE NEXT DAY AND WE AGREED TO MEET FOR DINNER that night. I went downtown to start jury selection in a truly pathetic theft case: my client, a homeless wino, was accused of stealing a ring from a corpse that had been dumped in an alley off Spring Street. The cops had tried to pinch him for the homicide but, failing that, took what they could get. The deputy district attorney was not anxious to try the case to a downtown jury likely to be composed of black and Latino jurors from crime-ridden neighborhoods who would perceive the trial as another instance of the system's misplaced priorities. The judge was equally unhappy at having his court tied up by what he had described in chambers as a "chickenshit case." As the jurors filed in, the DA passed me a note that read. "How about a drunk in public with time served?" I scribbled back, "OK, with no probation." She frowned, then shrugged, and asked to approach the bench. Ten minutes later, my man pled and the case was closed.

* * *

Leaving the court, I got tied up in traffic and was twenty minutes late to the restaurant where I was meeting Josh. The place was a typical Westside bistro, whitewashed walls, black lacquered chairs and tables, concrete floors and atonal music, like drips of rain, falling between syllables of trendy conversation. It was hard to believe that this was in the same city where dead bodies were dumped in alleys and looted for the price of a bottle of Tokay.

A pretty girl in a white Spandex dress pointed me toward Josh, who sat against the wall at a back table. He was wearing a black leather jacket over an Act Up T-shirt, black denim pants and clunky black shoes, that season's garb for the gay urban revolutionary. In my gray pinstripes I felt conspicuously Older Generation though, in fact, we were simply at opposite poles of the same generation.

"I'm sorry I'm late," I said, sitting down.

"I just got here myself," he said, sipping absently from a glass of white wine. Ordinarily, he refrained from drinking around me, and I was irritated at how quickly his habits were changing.

"You order yet?"

"No, I was waiting for you."

I grunted acknowledgment. We spent a couple of minutes on the hand-written menus and then gave our orders to the handsome waiter who, after he took it, told Josh, "Love your shoes. Doc Marten's?"

"Yeah, Zodiac's having a sale."

The waiter grinned, "Good deal."

I hadn't the faintest notion of what they were talking about. Sourly, I reflected that Steven would have understood. A busboy brought us water and I took a drink to wash down the bile before trying to hold a conversation.

"I'm glad to see you," Josh said. "Sorry about the misunderstanding yesterday."

It was hard to sustain my irritability, but I tried. "What misunderstanding; I was just a little late."

"No," he said, "not that part. I'm sorry I didn't tell you Steven would be there. I wanted to introduce you."

"Why?"

The force of my hostility startled him, but only for a moment. He said, "Because I care about both of you."

"Sorry, I don't mean to be a bitch. I'm just tired, and this isn't a situation I've ever been in before. I don't know the rules."

"There aren't rules, Henry," he said. He picked up his wine and drank some nervously. "I know it's naive but I thought if you met him you wouldn't be so mad at me."

"I'm not mad at you," I replied.

"If you were any tenser, you'd explode."

He was right; my shoulders were hunched to my ears. I took a long breath and dropped them. "He's younger than me by ten years and he has the kind of body you see advertising 976 numbers," I said. "I don't see that meeting him would make me feel better."

"You're not giving me a lot of credit if you think that that's what this is all about," he said. A peal of faked laughter cut through the chatter around us. "I've never had any complaints about our sex life."

"Oh, thanks."

He rolled the stem of the wine glass between his long fingers. "Could you try not to be such an asshole, Henry?"

"Maybe you'd better tell me why it is you asked me here while there's still time to cancel our orders."

He got up and started out of the room, bumping against the packed tables. I got up and hurried after him. I found him in the parking lot leaning against his car, crying.

"Josh."

"You think this is some cheap faggot farce, don't you," he said thickly. "This is my goddamned life."

"It's my life, too."

He wiped his nose on the sleeve of his jacket. "Just listen to me.

I don't want to die, Henry. I want to be like everyone else. I want my seventy-five years or whatever, but I know I'm not going to have them and it makes me crazy." He tipped his head back and swallowed hard. "I can't help resenting you. You're going to be alive after I'm dead and you'll find someone else." He drew a deep breath. "It's not fair. I had to get away from you. I had to get away from my own resentment."

"This isn't the way," I said, moving toward him. I put my arms around him and pulled him close. "There's never going to be anyone else."

I heard the 'thwack' of the newspaper against the front door and opened my eyes. Josh lay beside me on his stomach, his face turned away from me. He was a restless sleeper and the sheets had fallen away from him, exposing the full length of his body. He was a little man, five-eight on a good day, he liked to say, three inches shorter than me, but in far better shape. He had taken an anatomy class and learned the names of the muscles. Taking my hand, he would place it somewhere on his body and say, "This is a deltoid. This is a latissimus dorsi." The ripple of muscle beneath smooth skin was like a slow burning fire.

It was the mystery of my sexual nature that a body which was the mirror image of mine could be so compelling and feel so unfamiliar, as if it belonged to a separate gender. When I was younger, it had seemed urgent to unravel this mystery because I believed that if it could be explained, the haters would stop hating us. Now I believed that they had no more right to an explanation about me than I did about them and, in any case, they would find other reasons to hate. Now I was simply grateful for his body beside me, known and unknown.

I kissed the nape of his neck and got up, put on my pants and went out to get the paper. Tossing it on the kitchen table, I started the coffee, poured myself a glass of orange juice, swallowed some vitamins. I unrolled the newspaper and the headline stopped me cold: SENATOR PEÑA MURDERED, Legislator Shot to Death in Restaurant Parking Lot.

I started reading:

> Popular politician Agustin Peña who represented East Los Angeles for the past fifteen years in the state senate was shot to death in the parking lot of an Eastside restaurant late last night. Peña, who had been dining with his family at La Playa Azul on First Street, was killed while walking to his car.
> ' No one else was injured. Although he was rushed to a nearby hospital, he died early this morning. Police have no suspects . . .

Although the story went on at some length, all the known facts were in that first paragraph: a killing with no motive, no suspects, and no witnesses. The rest was the usual police disinformation, speculation that he might have come upon a car burglar who shot in panic; things the cops said when they didn't have anything. My first thought was about Michael Ruiz, who was, after a fashion, my client. I picked up the phone and called. Edith Rosen had just arrived.

"Do you know about Gus?" I asked.

"It's horrible, Henry. It's just horrible," she said. "I can hardly believe it."

"Does Chuck know?"

"He was at the hospital with the family," she said.

"What about Michael Ruiz?"

"Michael was here last night," she said. "He had nothing to do with it."

"Is he being a little more cooperative around there?"

"He knows it's his last chance," she said evasively.

"I hope that means yes."

"The police don't seem to know anything about who killed Gus," she said.

"That won't last long. Peña was an important man, they'll do everything they can to catch his killer as quickly as possible."

"I hope they do," she said, sincerely. "I have to go, Henry. Perhaps we'll talk later."

* * *

I was uneasy about the conversation, but in the absence of any reason for suspicion, I had to let it go. I went back to the paper. On the inside pages were statements from prominent politicians expressing shock at the killing. My old friend, Inez Montoya, now a city councilwoman, went on at length about the loss to the Chicano community. Her effusiveness surprised me. Although she had once worked for Gus, he had opposed her candidacy for city council and she still spoke of him with bitterness. I didn't know his family to call and express my own regret, so I called Inez instead.

"I can't talk now," she said, with her usual abruptness. "I'm on my way to Graciela."

"Peña's wife? Are you two friends?"

"I was always closer to her. Listen, will you be my date to the funeral?"

"Sure," I said.

"Fine, I'll call you with the details."

"Hi." Josh appeared at the doorway, naked, scratching his chest. "I smelled coffee." He looked at me. "What's wrong, Henry?"

"Gus Peña was murdered last night," I said, indicating the paper.

Josh came over and glanced at the headline. "Peña," he said. "Homophobic pig. You know he refused to sponsor a bill to fund a minority AIDS project in East LA? He actually said he wouldn't be party to promoting homosexuality and drug use."

I looked at the picture of Peña in the paper, tuxedoed, smiling. "No, I didn't know that," I said.

He yawned and looked at the article. "They shot him, huh? Assassination, you think?"

"I guess that's always a possibility with a politician, though a state senator doesn't exactly wield great power."

"You never know," Josh said. "They pass the laws. He could've really pissed someone off."

The gangs, I thought, and their defenders, like Tomas Ochoa.

"Maybe it was Act Up," he said.

"You're not serious."

"We talk about it sometimes," he said, pouring himself a cup of coffee and heading to the refrigerator for milk. "Like, if you're dying of AIDS, why not take out a few politicians. Hey, we're out of milk."

"Sorry, I haven't bought it since . . . " I let that sentence hang. "Would you do that?" I asked.

"Only if I had a crack at Jesse Helms." He closed the refrigerator. "Keep buying milk, OK?"

The morning TV news was full of Gus's murder. Since the police couldn't report any leads, most of it was filler. At one point, Tomas Ochoa was interviewed as an expert on Chicano politics to explain the significance of Peña's murder. He used the opportunity to rail against Peña's anti-gang bill and warn the police against scapegoating the gangs. Inez Montoya was interviewed at Peña's house. The message she delivered to the police was that any delay in capturing Peña's killer would be viewed as an insult to the Latino community. She brushed aside questions of whether the killing was an assassination. "It was just some punk," she snapped. The family was not available to the press, which had to content itself with shots of Mrs. Peña being led to a waiting car by her son.

I got dressed and went to my office, half-expecting a message from someone in Peña's office since I had been scheduled to meet with him that afternoon. No one had bothered calling. It was a moot point anyway.

I called my investigator Freeman Vidor about a witness he was trying to locate for me. We got around to Peña's murder. Freeman, as usual, had inside information from his contacts in the police department on which he'd served for a dozen years before the racism of his brother officers finally drove him out.

"Ballistics thinks it was an Uzi," he said. "They found a dozen shell casings in the lot."

"That was some car burglar," I said.

"It wasn't a car burglar. You know who likes Uzis, the gang-bangers. Looks to me like a drive-by shooting."

"That's Varrio Nuevo territory," I said. The names and territories of the Chicano gangs were familiar to every criminal defense attorney who worked downtown. The archrivals of the Varrio Nuevo gang were called the Dogtown Locos. I mentioned this to Freeman.

"That's who I would put my money on."

"Even in the dark, Peña couldn't have looked like a gang member."

"Maybe there was someone else in the lot," he conjectured.

"Maybe they expected to find Peña," I said.

"Hey, didn't he run over someone up in Sacramento a couple of months ago? Maybe the guy had family in LA and it was a revenge shooting."

"Hmm. If I were the cops I'd at least look into it," I replied.

"You know what else is kind of interesting," Freeman said, "I heard the toxo report came back showing the senator was drunk."

"Jesus," I said. "After that speech he made last week." Not to mention the little speech he'd made to me afterwards.

"I guess he just couldn't keep off the hootch," Freeman said. "You know the guy?"

"He'd asked me to represent him up in Sacramento," I said.

"There's one fee you won't be getting."

▲

CHAPTER

SEVEN

▼

THE SATURDAY AFTER PEÑA'S MURDER WAS MAY 5, CINCO DE MAYO, A holiday commemorating Mexico's victory over the invading French army in 1862. In Los Angeles, it was the occasion for the Chicano community to display the cultural nationalism that lay just below the surface of a city that retained its Spanish place names but had otherwise entombed its origins beneath the Hollywood sign. With Peña's murder, the celebrations took on an edge. There was a rally downtown in Peña's honor that turned violent when rival gangs starting shooting each other up. At another rally in East LA, Tomas Ochoa attempted to incite the crowd against the police who'd been called out to prevent further gang violence. Even at the pricey Chicano Bar Association dinner I attended on Saturday night there was muttering about whether the police were pursuing their investigation with the same dispatch as they would have had Peña been an Anglo politician. To me, this was bad news. The more pressure that was put on the police, the likelier it was that they would scapegoat someone. By the time Monday morning rolled around, the day of Peña's funeral, the city was braced for violence.

I made my way across a police barricade to City Hall where I was picking up Inez Montoya for the short walk to the church where the funeral was being held. A metal detector had been set up at the entrance. Inside, police officers were posted beneath the eight civic virtues, shiftily eyeing the few bureaucrats who had bothered showing up for work that day. Inez was on the phone in her inner office, so I waited outside.

It had been at Inez's table at a fund-raising dinner two years earlier where I'd first met Gus Peña. He'd come over to congratulate his one-time administrative assistant on her election to the city council out of the same district which he represented in the state senate. There had been a certain amount of condescension in the gesture, which, Inez had later told me, pretty much summed up his attitude toward women in general.

I'd known Inez for years, from her days, and mine, as public defenders. I'd worked up north at the time, and she was in Los Angeles. We'd met at a statewide meeting of the CPDA, California Public Defenders' Association, a group loftily dedicated to promoting the best legal services possible for indigent criminal defendants, back in the days when young lawyers thought this was a worthy goal. A long time ago, obviously.

We'd gotten drunk together—I was still drinking then—and she had tried to seduce me. She'd always had terrible luck with men. But we'd stayed friends and I'd watched her career, helping in whatever small ways I could, as she made her way through the political maelstrom on brains and guts and a passionate commitment to the disenfranchised. She was an altogether admirable, if sometimes scary, human being.

As I sat leafing though an issue of *Hispanic* magazine, I heard her shouting in her office.

"Don't give me any bureaucratic excuses," she was saying. "This guy's the worst slumlord in the city."

One of her staffers looked at me and smiled. From within her office, she growled, "Yeah, well you are the Building and Safety Department, aren't you?" After a moment's pause, she resumed her tirade. "Well if I don't have an answer by the end of the day I'm going to haul your ass down here to explain why." There was a jangle as she slammed down the receiver.

"I guess you can go in now," her aide told me.

"Thanks." I went to the door and knocked.

"What?" she demanded.

I pushed the door open and said, "Building and Safety inspector, ma'am."

She smiled, "Was I being a little loud? A little unladylike?"

"You ready to go pay your respects to Gus?"

She pulled a cigarette out of the pack on her desk and lit it, sucking greedily. "Is it time, already? Do I look OK?"

In her dark suit, her hair pulled back and tied with one of her trademark ribbons, she could have passed for a schoolgirl.

"You look fine."

She got up and hoisted her purse over her shoulder. "Let's go, then."

"This place looks like a scene out of that Costa-Gavras movie, *State of Siege*," I said as we crossed the rotunda, past the unsmiling countenances of the police guards.

"Oh, them," she said, dismissively. "It's safer than working the streets."

Outside, it was hot and clear, the early signs of another scorching summer. The trees on the grounds of City Hall sagged listlessly. The grass had been allowed to die, a concession to the drought, but it was still heavily populated in equal measure by street people and city workers eating lunch. A grizzled old man stood on the corner of Main and First, shrieking passages from the Bible, a Styrofoam cup balanced on his head. As we approached him, he stopped in mid-imprecation, reached for the cup and took a drink from it.

She put her arm through mine and said, "I've always wondered what he had in that cup."

"God's work is thirsty work, I guess."

"LA, don't you love it?"

"It got to be a hot weekend," I said, not referring to the weather.

"I know, I know. I've spent the last five days trying to keep people in my district calm."

"Tomas Ochoa didn't help matters."

"That shit," she said.

"I saw you on TV last night talking about Gus," I said, pulling her toward me to avoid a broken bottle of Gallo port on the sidewalk. On the tube, she had praised Peña as a friend of the poor and leader in the continuing fight for the civil rights of all people. "Did you mean it?"

"You're so cynical, Henry. You should go into politics." Waving away a panhandler, she said, "Of course I meant it. Gus had an excellent record on social legislation. In his own way, he was a powerful advocate for the community. The fact that he was also an asshole is neither here nor there. Besides," she added, thoughtfully, "there aren't so many Chicano politicians that we can afford to lose one."

"Who do you think killed him?"

She wasn't listening. We'd crossed First and were heading down Main, past boarded-up storefronts that reeked of urine, and a parking lot where the homeless lived in tents made out of plastic garbage bags and cardboard boxes.

"Look at this," she said, indignation darkening her voice. "In one of the richest cities in the world people live like this." She looked at me, frowning. "Gus wore thousand-dollar suits, but he knew what it was like to be poor. Unlike the gringos who run this town."

"I'm on your side," I reminded her.

Traffic had been diverted around the church, and a line of black limousines was parked alongside it. Police officers patrolled the area keeping the crowd at bay. I began to hear chanting. As we approached I saw that it was coming from a contingent of black Tshirted, placard-waving Act Up members. One of them read, "Save the Minority AIDS Project." Others repeated in Spanish the group's motto, Silence = Death.

Separated from them by a line of cops was another group, mostly Chicano kids, holding up their own placards denouncing the police. Some of them had started shouting "Faggots," and "Queers," at the Act Up contingent. I thought I caught a glimpse of Ochoa among them.

"What's Act Up doing here?" Inez asked.

"They're pushing funding for the Minority AIDS Project," I said, repeating what Josh had told me. "They figured there'd be a big contingent of politicians at the funeral."

"It looks to me like there's going to be a fight," she said.

We'd come to the police line. I looked over to where the cops had contained the Act Up people, searching to see if Josh was there. He was, one hand raised in a fist in the air, and the other around Steven Wolfe's waist. He saw me and began walking forward, but a black cop pushed him back with the edge of his baton.

"There's Josh," I said, pulling her with me as I hurried over to him.

Josh was arguing with the cop, Steven coming up behind him, when we got there.

"Excuse me, officer," I said. "This is a friend of mine."

The cop looked me up and down in my black suit, and glanced at Inez. "Sorry, sir, the demonstrators have to stay behind the lines."

"I just want to talk to him," I said.

"Officer," Inez said, pulling her wallet out of her purse. "I'm with him." She flipped her wallet open, showing some kind of badge. He looked at it.

"OK, but just you," he said to Josh, letting him through. Steven smiled at me with unmistakable disdain.

"Hi, Inez," Josh said. "What was that you showed him?"

"City council members carry a badge," she said. "It gets us out of traffic tickets. You want to come inside with us?"

He shook his head. "Hi, Henry."

"Hi. It looks like there's going to be trouble here, Josh," I said, indicating the Chicano demonstrators.

"The cops will keep them away from us."

"I'd feel better if you came inside." After a moment, I said, "You could bring Steven, too."

"Sure, if you don't mind that we disrupt the funeral."

Inez said, "That would not be a good idea."

Josh touched my lapel. "Then I guess we better stay out here."

"Why don't we both go home, then," I said.

He shook his head, "Those days are over, Henry. You can't protect me anymore."

Inez tugged my elbow. "Henry, let's go."

"See you later," Josh said, and kissed me. "Bye, Inez."

"Good-bye, Josh. Keep your head down." As we walked away she asked, "What was that all about?"

"Marital discord," I replied, and left it at that.

Uniformed cops swarmed the entrance to the cathedral. As at City Hall, we had to pass through a metal detector. A tall man who looked like a cop in plainclothes called over to her. "Councilwoman Montoya?" We walked over to him. "Fred Hanley," he said. "LAPD anti-terrorist squad. If you'd step this way, I'll have someone show you to your seat."

"What's going on here?" she asked.

"Just a precaution, ma'am," he said, sounding exactly like Sergeant Friday. He handed us over to another plainclothesman who took us into the church and sat us four rows back from the altar. I could make out the backs of the heads of Peña's wife and children in the front. Gus's casket was on a flower-strewn dais. It had been left half-open, "half-couch," in the argot of morticians with which I had become more familiar than I had ever wanted to be in the past few years of burying friends who'd died of AIDS. I could make out Gus's stern profile.

The service began.

As far as I was concerned, the Catholic Church was just another totalitarian political entity, like the Communist Party or IBM, but I had to admit, it put on a good show. As I watched the theatrics unfold, I thought of Gus Peña. Over the past five days, the news stories about Gus had filled in the holes in my knowledge about him.

He was the son of Mexican immigrants and, as Inez had said, he knew what it was like to be poor. After high school, he'd joined the military, and done a tour of duty in Vietnam. Upon his return, he'd come back to the city and put himself through college and law school. In the sixties, he'd worked with Chavez's farmworkers. Later, he'd come home to East LA where he opened up a law practice and began building the foundations of his political career.

I'd grown up in a place as poor as East LA, and I knew what he'd bucked to turn himself into the suave politician he had become. Inez was also right that he had never forgotten his roots. That in itself was an accomplishment; self-made men had a tendency to generalize their experience into a sour kind of bigotry against the poor. Peña could have escaped into the reaches of the upper-middle-class, the token "Hispanic" partner at some big downtown law firm, but he hadn't. Having had to work twice as hard for what he deserved on merit alone, he'd developed a kind of rage, like an extra set of muscles, propelling him through life. The rage never went away. There was never enough to reward you for what you had suffered. And you never, ever, forgot you were an outsider, no matter how expensive your suits.

I could imagine all this because I had traversed the same trajectory. The difference was, being homosexual as well as Chicano, I'd had to learn a level of self-acceptance that mitigated my anger. Having had to overcome my own self-hatred, I couldn't sustain hatred toward other people very long, not even the people who ran the Catholic Church, though God knows they deserved it. This inability to hate didn't make me virtuous; it was just part of who I was.

I wondered if Peña had known who he was when he died, or if he'd died in the rage, like my father, his best instincts warring with his worst. No wonder he needed to drink.

"My father was a man with a lot to do."

I looked up at the altar where Gus Peña's son was standing at the podium, looking remarkably composed and touchingly young. I'd only half-listened to the parade of luminaries who'd been eulogizing Gus in phrases so general they could have applied to any politician, but this boy—Tino?—had my attention.

"When I was a kid, I resented the fact that he was so busy," the boy said. "He wasn't like other dads. I guess part of me missed that, but when I got older I understood why he was so busy. His work was the people's work." He paused, looked down at the casket, and then at the crowded church. "Dad, the people didn't forget you. They're here today." He lowered his head, composing himself. "And we're here, too, Dad. Mom, Angela, and me. To say good-bye." He bent forward slightly, weeping. Next to me, I heard Inez's low sobbing, too. The boy raised his head and continued. "My father believed in the God of justice," he said. "Justice for everyone. I hope God will judge him justly and treat him with mercy. Good-bye, Dad."

In the stillness that followed, the chants of the demonstrators outside echoed through the church.

"Are you going to the interment?" I asked Inez when we were out on the sidewalk. The crowd was breaking up. The demonstrators were gone, but the police remained in force.

Inez dabbed her eyes with my handkerchief. "No, I've got to get back to the office. You?"

"No, I don't think so. I'll walk you back."

Fred Hanley, the LAPD officer, came up and said, "Councilwoman, one of my men will drive you to City Hall."

She looked at me impatiently. "What is going on here? Why's the anti-terrorist squad out? And don't bullshit me."

"Yes, ma'am," Hanley said. "We have some reason to believe that Senator Peña was killed by a terrorist group that calls itself the Dogtown Locos."

"That's the name of a street gang," I said.

"Yes, sir," Hanley replied. "I'm sorry I can't say more. If you'd come with me, Councilwoman."

"Go on," I said. "I'll be all right. Call me later."

Inez nodded and went off with Hanley, whispering fiercely.

"Henry." Edith Rosen was walking toward me, her hair covered with a black scarf. "I didn't see you earlier."

"It was a full house," I replied. "How are you doing?"

"I need to talk to you," she said. "It's very important."

"Sure. Have you eaten lunch?"

"What I could really use," she said, removing her scarf, "is a drink."

CHAPTER

EIGHT

▲

▼

AT THE COMMODORE PERRY ROOM IN THE NEW OTANI, A GLASS WALL separated the bar from the Japanese Garden on the other side. A miniature footbridge forded a trickling stream shaded by small red-leaved plum trees. Inside, a big-screen Toshiba TV broadcast a soccer match from Buenos Aires and a lone cocktail waitress dressed in a black-and-gold kimono shuffled among the mostly empty tables filling little glass bowls with salted dried peas and rice sticks. I nursed a Diet Coke while, between sips of white wine, Edith Rosen told me she had lied to me about Michael Ruiz's whereabouts the night Peña was killed.

"I got a call around eleven from the counselor on duty," she explained, "telling me that Michael had left the house sometime earlier that night."

"Don't you have to sign out?"

"There's a big AA meeting at the house from eight-thirty to ten," she said. "Everyone goes outside to smoke on the break. He kept going. It wasn't until bed check they found he was missing."

"When did he come back?"

"Around midnight," she replied. "The counselor was supposed to write him up, but I told her to hold off until I had a chance to talk to him."

"And of course the next morning you found out that Gus had been murdered," I said. "And you told me that Michael had been at the house the night before."

"Look, Henry, I didn't think the two things had anything to do with each other," she insisted.

"Then why did you lie to me?"

"I didn't want to complicate things before I'd had a chance to talk to him."

"And what did he say when you did?"

"He said he went to see a movie," she replied. "He told me the name of the theater, the movie, the time it started and when it was over. I called the theater. They confirmed it."

"They confirmed seeing him?"

"It didn't seem necessary to ask," she replied brusquely.

"Did you write him up for taking off?"

"No," she said, looking into her drink.

"Why are you telling me this?"

"He took off again this morning," she said, lifting her face. "Just cleared out."

"What happened?"

"The police were at the house, asking questions about Gus. They came in to talk to me but I told them I couldn't say anything without violating the therapist-patient privilege—"

I cut in. "Did they want to know about Michael?"

"No, about Gus. I was his therapist, too. They wanted to know if he'd mentioned having received any death threats. That kind of thing."

"That kind of thing you could have told them," I said.

"I don't talk about my clients, period," she snapped. "Anyway, after they left, I saw Michael standing in the hallway. I think he must've seen them leaving my office. A little later, he missed group. That's when they found he was gone."

"Do you have any idea of where he might be?"

She shook her head. "I tried his parents and his grandmother. They didn't know."

"You still think this has nothing to do with Peña's murder?"

"I don't know what to think," she said quietly, and finished her drink.

I studied her kind, plain face for a moment. She looked as if she had lost a child. "Edith, why did you cover for Michael? It seems out of character for someone who takes her ethical obligations so seriously."

"One of my children got involved with drugs," she said, after a moment.

"You're married?"

"Divorced. We had two kids, a boy and a girl. It was my son who got caught up in drugs." She picked up her glass, saw it was empty, put it down again. "I really didn't understand because he seemed so well adjusted, and we were comfortable, our family, I mean. Of course, there was the usual tension, but there is in every family. I started looking for answers. Eventually, it led me back to school in psychology." She looked at me. "I was almost fifty, and my husband thought I was crazy, obsessed. I suppose he was right."

"Did you find your answers?" I asked.

"Some, I found some. Too late for Roger, though. He overdosed."

"I'm sorry."

"You know," she said, "I've seen hundreds of clients, all shapes, sizes and ages. I never knew that I was looking for Roger in them until I found Michael. Do you understand now, Henry? I wanted to change the ending."

"I understand completely," I said. "I'd like to change a few endings, too. I think you've just convinced me that it's not in my power."

"I have to get back to the house," she said, rising. "It's possible that Michael's with some of his gang friends. Do you think you could find that out?"

I thought of Tomas Ochoa. "I can try."

"Thank you, Henry."

"If he gets in touch with you, let me know immediately. By the way, what was the name of the theater Michael said he went to?"

"The Los Feliz," she said. "It's in walking distance of the house."

Driving back to my office, I called Inez Montoya to find out what further information she had managed to wrest from Fred Hanley, the Sergeant Friday clone, about gang involvement in Peña's murder.

"You know what it is," she said scornfully. "Over the weekend, the cops started seeing Dogtown *placasos* with Peña's name in it."

"What did the graffiti say?"

"'Peña *puto*,'" she quoted.

"How is calling Gus a queer claiming responsibility for killing him?" I asked.

"They told me it was the first time they've ever seen a politician's name show up in the *placasos*."

Just as she was speaking, I passed a building on Beverly whose wall was covered with spray-painted *placas*, filled with numbers and names in the serpentine script legible only to the gangbangers. The *placas* were a way of marking territory and trading insults. I, too, had never heard it used for political commentary.

"I don't think the cops are telling you everything they know," I said.

"Why should they?" she scoffed. "I'm only one of their employers."

"Maybe you could press them for more."

I heard her yelling something and then a door slammed shut. She came back on the line, "What's your interest?"

"You represent the same district that Peña did," I pointed out.

"If I were you, I'd be concerned about the gangs turning into political terrorists."

"Now you're beginning to sound like Ochoa," she said.

I said, "I have to make another call."

I got Tomas between classes. He didn't sound particularly happy to hear from me. When I brought up Gus's murder, I got about the response that I'd expected.

"Good riddance to bad rubbish," he said. "Listen, with that homicide charge hanging over him, getting killed was probably a good career move."

"It was certainly good for your career, Tomas. You've been on TV almost every night since he was killed."

"Listen, Rios, I'm busy. What do you want?"

I slowed for a red light. "I want to trade information with you."

That got a guarded, "What information?"

"You first," I said, stopping at the light. A man standing on the corner selling sacks of oranges shook one hopefully in my direction. I shook my head. "You're always hyping the gangs Tomas, but do you actually have any ties to them?"

"Why?"

"Because I have a client who I suspect may be involved with the gangs, but I need to know for sure."

"Ask him," Tomas said.

I accelerated through the green light. "He's disappeared," I said. "That's the problem. I want to know if he's with them."

"And what do you have to trade, Rios?"

"A warning," I said.

"Yeah? What?"

"The cops are going to start a sweep, if they haven't already." The Los Feliz theater came into sight.

"That's not news," he said. "They're out there every night."

"I'm talking about mass arrests," I said. "The day after Gus was killed the Governor signed his anti-gang bill with an urgency clause that put it into effect immediately. That's what the cops will be using." I pulled over just down the street from the theater. "What about it, Tomas, will you help me find my client?"

"What's his name?"

"Michael Ruiz," I said.

"When and where will the cops start their sweep?"

"Dogtown territory," I said. "Tonight, if they haven't already started."

"How do you know this?" he asked suspiciously.

"No, now it's your turn. Help me find Michael Ruiz."

"There are two hundred gangs in LA," he said. "You expect me to ask each one of them?"

"Only the ones that operate out of East LA. Try Dogtown and Varrio Nuevo."

"Maybe," he said.

It occurred to me that he hadn't asked me why the cops were coming down on the Dogtown gang. Maybe he already knew.

The girl at the Los Feliz had been working the night Gus was killed, but she didn't remember selling a ticket to a Chicano boy with a tear-drop tattoo. I thanked her and glanced up at the marquee. The Los Feliz was showing *Terminator 2*.

Although much had happened since my first session with Raymond Reynolds a week earlier, when I sat down in his gray office I wanted to pick up where we had left off, talking about my father. I announced this to Reynolds who smiled faintly, and said, "You've overcome your resistance to talking about mommy and daddy?"

"Don't gloat," I said, marveling at how comfortable I felt talking to this stranger about matters I had seldom discussed with anyone, but then, there was something about this process that seemed distantly familiar.

"Seriously, Henry, what happened this week that makes it important for you to talk about him?"

"Two things," I replied. "I went to a funeral this morning and heard a son talking about his father, and then later, I was talking to someone about changing endings. It made me think about my father's death."

"What about it?"

"I was in college," I said, "a sophomore. It was September, and I'd just turned nineteen. I hadn't been home since Christmas. My mother called me and told me my father was dying. I hadn't even known he was sick." I closed my eyes, remembering that clear September afternoon, standing in the hallway of the dorm. Going home was the last thing I wanted to do, but I went anyway. "He was dying of stomach cancer," I said. "He looked like someone who'd been in a concentration camp."

"What did you feel?" Reynolds asked, softly.

"I was shocked," I said. "And surprised. Shocked by the way he looked. Surprised that he was dying, surprised that he was mortal, after all."

"You didn't think he was mortal?"

"I didn't think he was human," I replied. "He seemed so big and his fury was bottomless. He was a whirlwind, like the Old Testament God, or something, ripping through my life, uprooting me, tossing me around. How could someone like that die?"

"That's a powerful image," he observed.

I looked out the slats of the blinds that covered the windows at the narrow bands of sky: red, orange, blue. When I was small the sky frightened me because it never changed, it was always that enormous dome of light or darkness, and I was afraid that I would be little forever, and in terror of the giant who was my father. The only prayer I had as a kid was for time to pass.

"I was glad he was dying. I thought I'd finally be free."

"Free from what?"

"From being afraid of him, from disappointing him, from never measuring up to this idea of what a man should be."

"Did he know you were gay?"

"I hardly knew myself at that age," I said, still looking out the window. The sky was darkening. "Growing up, I was sensitive and strong-willed. It was a combination that didn't make sense to his notions of being male. He thought I was simply weak and disobedient."

"And after he died, did that free you?"

"I live with his judgments of me," I said.

"And perhaps," Reynolds said, "you live out his judgments of you."

I looked at him. "What do you mean?"

"You lead an admirable life, Henry, but I wonder how much of it really gives you any satisfaction."

"That's not something I think about. There's too much to be done."

"Too much wrong to right?" he asked, with a trace of amusement in his voice.

"I just don't think the point of life is to sit beneath a tree and await enlightenment."

"I'm not suggesting you renounce the life you've made for yourself, just that you become more conscious of it."

"Why?" I asked skeptically.

"To discover your motives in having chosen it," he said, folding his hands in his lap like a little Buddha.

That night I dreamed about him, for the first time in years and years. I was back in the hospital room. His eyes glittered above his respirator. They were the last fully alive part of him, and I watched him focus on me as I entered the room. I sat down on the edge of the bed, trying to think of something to say to him. Then, he gripped my arm with fingers as bony as talons but with no

more strength than a child and began making choking noises, trying to speak. I leaned toward him. He was saying, "Don't let them
know."

I woke up in a fury that the last thing on earth he had asked me
was to keep secret how he had terrorized me, and that I had.

▲

CHAPTER

NINE

▼

WHEN I WOKE A SECOND TIME IT WAS MORNING BUT I FELT AS IF I hadn't slept at all. I lay in bed looking at the familiar objects that furnished the room as if seeing them for the first time, and I felt lost in the life which they represented. When I was a child I had worked hard at making myself invisible and I emerged from it without an identity. Over the years, I had crafted one for myself, and now Raymond Reynolds was telling me it was all wrong. It was still better than not existing at all. I needed to talk to someone. Various names entered my head: Reynolds, Josh, even Edith Rosen, and then I remembered Timothy Taylor to whom I'd owed a call since Cullen's service. I picked up the phone and dialed his number.

"Good morning," he chirped.

I hesitated. "Tim, it's Henry Rios."

"What's wrong, honey, you sound like your best friend just died."

"No," I said, drawing the covers over me. "I had a bad dream and I woke up kind of shaky."

"Why don't you tell me about it."

I related my dream, feeling a little foolish, but Timothy listened without making a sound.

"You know," he said, "my father was the first person who ever called me a queer. I think I was eight at the time." He giggled, "And I hadn't even done anything yet. I mean, I didn't actually start sucking cock until I was, oh, eight and a half."

I smiled for the first time that day. He continued, "I didn't even know what he meant, but I still wanted to kill him for saying it. But being a certified sissy, I ended up almost killing myself instead. All those years sitting in queer bars drinking out of anger at that prick. I'd show him who was a queer. After a few drinks, of course, I could've cared less. Tell me something, Henry, when you were drinking did you think much about your dad?"

I thought back. Between the time I was seventeen when I had my first drink at a kegger, and landing in an alcoholic ward when I was thirty-four, I had had almost nothing to do with my family.

"No," I said. "Not much."

"I didn't think so," he said. "I bet you've always been the strong silent type of drunk. But back to me, when I got sober I was still pissed at the old man, but I couldn't get drunk about it anymore. I just had to sit still and let it pass. Do you get my point, or am I being too subtle?"

"I understand," I said. "I'm not sure why this is all coming up now, though."

"Mmmm," he said. "For being such a smart man, you are remarkably dense about some things."

"Gee, thanks, Tim. I guess now you'll explain it to me."

"Right you are," he replied. "Sister Mary Timothy explains it all. Look, doll, your boyfriend has just walked out on you and taken up with another guy. That's what's churning your butter."

"You have a gift for the tawdry."

"Flatterer."

"I don't see how the two things are related."

"Dumb, dumb, dumb," he said with mock exasperation. "Honey, do you really think you have separate sets of emotions? If you're hurt and pissed at Josh for leaving you, it's going to bring up every other time some man," he drew out the word into two syllables— mah-an— "hurt you and pissed you off. And it sounds like your dad went to the same school of child rearing that mine did." He paused for a moment, and when he spoke again, his tone was serious. "You know, Henry, we're the only people who get born into the enemy camp. I mean, black babies get born into black families, Jewish babies get born into Jewish families, but gay babies, we get born into straight families. How we survive it at all is a miracle."

"I don't think my father knew I was gay."

"Henry, darling, why do you think he was so mad at you? Something about you made him very unhappy."

"I'm sure there was a lot about me that made him unhappy," I replied. "I'm not sure it was being gay. I didn't know that about myself until I was sixteen, but you are right about one thing. He let me know I wasn't his kind of man."

"No," he said, "but look at you. You're smart, sensitive, successful—"

"Trustworthy, loyal and obedient."

"OK, then don't take a compliment, as long as you understand what I'm saying. There's nothing wrong with the kind of man you are."

I laughed. "That means a lot from someone who dressed up last Halloween as Barbara Bush."

"Bitch," he replied. "Oh, maybe the bouffant was a tad overdone, but I thought I carried it off rather well. Now, can I finish?"

"Please."

"There's nothing wrong with the kind of man you are," he repeated. "Let go of what your father wanted you to be and maybe you'll stop hating him so much."

After a moment, I asked, "How did you get so smart, Timmy?"

"Kicking and screaming," he replied. "And I have the scars to prove it."

"What about your dad? You ever make your peace with him?"

"Well," he said, cautiously, "we're never going to be the Beav and Mr. Cleaver, but we talk. I've got to run. Call me later if you need to."

"Thanks, Tim."

"Bye, doll."

I got up, suddenly ravenous. In the kitchen I scrambled a couple of eggs with cheese, made a pot of coffee, toasted a slice of Italian bread that I spread with butter and marmalade, and set the table. I went out and picked up the paper. Buried on an inside page of the Metro section was a story about how the police had conducted a sweep of East LA the night before, using Gus Peña's anti-gang law to round up almost a hundred "suspected gang members."

When I got to work that morning, Tomas Ochoa had already called twice. Before I had a chance to return his calls, Emma came into the office, looking grim.

"Henry, there are a couple of cops outside who want to talk to you," she said.

"What about?"

"They said they wanted to speak to you privately," she sniffed.

"All right, send them back."

They dressed with conspicuous anonymity. The older of the two was a bald, haggard-looking man in a gray suit, white shirt, and a blue-and-gray tie. The younger was stocky, also in a gray suit and blue tie but he, in an impetuous moment, had chosen a blue shirt. They arranged themselves stolidly in the chairs in front of my desk and gave me a look that made me feel as if I were being patted down for weapons.

The older said, "I'm Detective Laverty and this is Detective Merrill. We'd like to talk to you about Senator Peña."

"Why? I hardly knew the man."

"You were at his funeral," Laverty said.

"What did you do, take pictures of everyone who came in?" I asked. Laverty decided to treat this as a joke, and smiled politely. "At any rate, half the city was at Gus Peña's funeral."

Merrill broke in. "Yeah, and we're talking to all of them."

Laverty threw him a look, then said to me, "Did you speak to the Senator the night of his death?"

"No, why do you ask?"

"We found your card on his desk."

"So what?"

"Can you tell us the circumstances under which you gave him your card?" he persisted.

"Not until you tell me why my business card is so interesting to you. Or are you going through his Rolodex?"

Laverty pulled out a notebook. "Senator Peña made two calls to you the night he was killed. The first call, to your office, was made at around 7:00 P.M. The second call was to your residence."

"You checked his outgoing calls? You must be stalled."

"It's routine," he replied.

"In that case, I'm sure his phone records must also show that he didn't reach anyone because I didn't talk to him that night."

Laverty pretended to consult his notes. "No, not at your office, but he did reach someone at your residence, and he was on the line for almost three minutes. You have an answering machine? You live with someone?"

I spoke quickly to conceal my surprise. "There was no message from Peña on my phone machine that night, and I live alone."

Without missing a beat, Laverty said, "Phone company shows another listing for your number. J. Mandel."

"He moved out."

"I see," Laverty said. We were all quiet for a moment. Finally, Laverty asked, "You know a woman named Edith Rosen?"

"You wouldn't ask the question if you didn't know the answer," I replied.

"You spoke to her the day after the Senator was killed," he said.

"Have you been at my phone records, too?"

Laverty cleared his throat. "We looked at them informally."

"You looked at them illegally."

"Counselor," Laverty said, "we're trying to find out who killed Senator Peña. We're obliged to follow every lead we have."

"Are you suggesting that Edith Rosen or I are involved in Gus's death?"

"We're just trying to find out if he said anything to anyone in the days before he was killed that could help us out."

"Gentlemen, I didn't talk to Gus Peña the night he was killed, and any conversation I had with Edith Rosen is privileged."

Laverty picked up on that immediately. "Miss Rosen a client of yours?"

"I've said as much as I'm going to, and now I have work to do."

They got up. No one offered to shake anyone's hand and no one said thank you either. After they left, I analyzed our little talk. It was clear that they didn't have much to go on, and I doubted if they knew about Michael Ruiz. Unfortunately, by claiming the privilege on my conversation with Edith, I'd supplied them with a lead. I called her to warn her.

"They were already out here this morning," she said. "They asked me the same questions they asked the first time and I gave them the same answer."

"You asserted the privilege."

"Yes, of course."

"Did they talk to Chuck?"

"Not as far as I know."

"Have you told Chuck about Michael's disappearance the night Gus was killed?"

"Yes," she replied. "He wasn't happy about it."

"Did you tell him you've claimed the privilege with the cops?"

"No, that's none of his business. What are you thinking, Henry?"

"I'm thinking that if you're claiming one privilege and I'm claiming another, the cops are going to conclude that we're hiding something."

"Those privileges exist to protect people," she said sternly.

"They see it differently," I remarked. "They'll probably come back to the house and try you again. If you stonewall them, they'll get around to Chuck, eventually. He'll tell them about Michael's threat on Peña's life."

After a moment, she asked, "What should I do?"

"If it's going to come out, you might as well tell them yourself."

"You know I can't do that."

"Would you rather that they hear Chuck's version?"

"It's a matter of principle."

I let it go. "Have you heard from Michael at all?"

"No, not a word."

"Let me know the moment you do."

I was still puzzled by the phone calls that the cops said Peña had made to me the night he was killed. I'd gone directly from court to dinner with Josh without stopping at home. The only other person who had a key to the house was Josh, and he had already been at the restaurant when I arrived. Then I remembered that when I'd sat down and apologized for being late, he had said . . .

"Josh," I said, when he came on the line after I exchanged a few minutes of small talk with his mother, "do you remember last Wednesday night, when we met for dinner?"

"Hi to you, too," he replied. "Yes, I'm fine. Thanks for asking."

"Sorry," I said. "I've got something on my mind."

"I can tell," he said.

I took a deep breath. "Josh, this is important."

"What's important?"

"The night we had dinner."

"What about it?"

"I remember that I apologized for being late, but you said, you'd just got there, too."

"So?"

"So you were also late."

"I told you," he said, "I had to stop at the house to pick up my leather jacket."

"You didn't tell me that," I said.

"You know I hate it when you use that lawyer-voice on me."

"Sorry," I said, wondering what the hell a lawyer-voice sounded like, but I decided now was not the time to pick a fight. "Did anyone call while you were at the house, just before you left?"

"How am I supposed to remem—oh, yeah. Someone did call. Some drunk."

"Some drunk?"

"I was on my way out when the phone rang and there was some drunk. I figured it was either one of your clients or someone you gave your name to at an AA meeting, so I tried to talk to him, but he was pretty loaded."

"Did he say his name?"

"No, he just started babbling. I was running late, so I hung up on him, figuring he would call you later, when he was sober. So what's the big deal?"

"It was Gus Peña," I said.

He was quiet for a moment. "Do you know what he wanted?"

"No," I said. "The police were here earlier and they told me he'd called. That's all I know."

"Sorry, I probably meant to tell you, but then we got into that fight."

"Do you remember anything that he said?"

"He asked for you, and I told him you weren't there. I asked him if he wanted to leave a message, and he started to babble. I was in a hurry, so I cut it short."

"He didn't say why he was calling?"

"Henry," he replied irritably, "I could barely understand him."

"All right, I don't mean to cross-examine you."

"Don't you?"

"Listen, Josh, why are you trying to pick a fight with me? After the other night, I thought we had a truce going."

"Maybe it's because I've had five years of calls like this," he said. "When you're working on a case nothing else matters."

"I've always made time for you."

"'Made time'," he repeated. "I don't have as much time as you do, Henry. I can't wait for an empty slot in your appointment book."

"What about tonight?"

"No," he said, "not tonight."

"Steven."

"Now who's trying to start a fight?"

"I just asked a question."

"That was a statement and, yes, Steven. Happy?"

"Excuse me," I said. "Was I using my lawyer-voice?"

He hung up.

I pushed my marital troubles out of my head and tried to think of why Gus Peña had called me on the night he was killed. I doubted that the reason was as simple as cancelling his appointment the next day. As far as everyone knew, Gus Peña was sober, so why would he have exposed the lie to me? The only plausible explanation was that he was in trouble. I itched to know what kind of trouble, but didn't know where to turn for an answer.

A moment later, the intercom buzzed. I picked up the phone, and Emma said, "Professor Ochoa's on the line. Do you want to talk to him?"

"I suppose I'd better," I said.

"You might tell him to learn some phone manners," she said, and put him on the line.

"Rios?"

"Sorry I didn't get back to you sooner."

"How did you know about the sweep last night?" he demanded.

"We were going to trade information as I recall," I said.

"They just picked people up off the street, and hauled them off to county," he continued in the same angry vein. "You working for the cops now?"

"If I were working for the cops, why would I have told you there was going to be a sweep?"

"To try to incriminate me," he replied. "You figured I'd get the word out to them and then the cops come after me. It's called entrapment."

"I could get lost trying to follow the twists in your thinking. All I want to know is where my client is."

"Yeah? Who is this Michael Ruiz? An undercover cop?"

"This isn't getting us anywhere."

"Why are the cops coming down on the *vatos?*"

"I think you know," I replied.

He hung up. A moment later, however, he called back. "Come to my office at four-thirty," he said, then hung up again.

▲

CHAPTER

TEN

▼

Tomas taught at Cal State Los Osos in a remote suburb in the San Fernando Valley. The campus had apparently been designed by the same architects the state retained to design its prisons: its buildings were a collection of concrete slabs linked by four-lane sidewalks that crossed yellowing strips of grass. All that kept the place from being completely depressing was the irrepressible energy of its students. From card tables set up outside the student union, decorated with homemade signs, they hawked causes from gay liberation to animal rights, handing out leaflets with boundless optimism. Walking past them made me feel very old.

Ochoa was waiting in his office, a grim little cubicle on the edge of the campus. On the wall was a faded poster calling for the expulsion of the Anglos from California. More recent posters proclaimed support for the PLO and commemorated thirty years of Castro in Cuba. Ochoa was a believer, and though I thought his beliefs were foolish, I had to envy his tenacity.

Floor to ceiling bookshelves were crammed with books in Spanish and English; tomes of history, political science, literature, philosophy, sociology, psychology, law. He regarded me suspiciously from a desk stacked high with papers as I perused his bookshelves.

"You have a lot of books here," I said, clearing some from the only other chair in the room. "I'm surprised you haven't come up with better answers."

"Better answers than what?"

I indicated the yellowing poster calling for a revolution. "Than this."

"I didn't ask you here to discuss politics," he replied. "What are the police after?"

"First you answer my question," I said. "Where's Michael Ruiz?"

"He's not a *vato*," he said.

"You know that for sure?"

"He's a wannabe," he replied dismissively. "A drug addict."

"That's never disqualified anyone from joining a gang."

"It's so easy for you to write them off," he said. "The same way you write off the rest of your heritage."

"The gangs are not my heritage. What about Michael?"

"He tried to hang with Dogtown, but he didn't have what it takes. He wasn't man enough," he added, pointedly.

"Do you know where he is?" I asked, ignoring him.

"I gave you your information, now it's your turn. What are the cops after?"

"Peña's shooting had all the marks of a drive-by," I said. "The cops think it was gang-related."

"That's ridiculous."

"You're the one who says the gangs are urban revolutionaries. Maybe they finally heard you."

He scowled. "Don't try to implicate me."

"You've done a pretty good job of that yourself," I said. "Running around giving speeches after Peña was killed. I saw that you nearly incited a riot Saturday night."

He looked alarmed. "Are the cops after me?"

"I don't know, Tomas, but I wouldn't be giving any more speeches if I were you."

"Jesus, I come up for tenure this year. What should I do, Rios?"

I got up, enjoying his discomfort. "Whatever Che Guevara would have done."

When I got to my car, the phone was ringing. It was Emma. She told me that Edith Rosen had called and said it was urgent that I get to SafeHouse. I thanked her and tried to call SafeHouse, but got a busy signal, and began the drive back into town.

"Is Edith Rosen here?" I asked the skinny kid with the shaved head loitering in the foyer at SafeHouse.

"No, man, the cops took her," he said.

"Where?"

He looked at me vacantly and shrugged. "Down to cop-land, man."

"What about Chuck Sweeny?"

"He went with her," the kid said, then lost interest and wandered off.

It took me a half-dozen calls to locate them at Parker Center, police headquarters downtown. Chuck Sweeney was waiting for me when I entered the building.

"We tried to call you before we came down here," he said, after I'd explained my purpose to the cop at the front desk.

"Just tell me what's going on."

"The police came to the house and wanted to talk to Edith. I told them that the presence of the police made some of the residents uncomfortable, so they suggested we come down here."

"Suggested, huh?"

"We want to cooperate, Henry," he said, with unblinkingly candid blue eyes. "We're good citizens."

"Who is this 'we'?" I asked him.

"People like you and me," he said, "recovering drunks, recovering addicts."

"Edith is neither," I pointed out. "She's a psychotherapist attempting to protect her client."

"It's a form of dishonesty," he replied. "If she knows something, she should tell it. A man's been murdered."

"And you've already convicted Michael Ruiz for the crime, haven't you, Chuck. Haven't you heard of the presumption of innocence?"

He smiled his P.R. smile and said, "Sure, that's what criminals hide behind when they get caught."

The cop at the desk told me I could go back to where Edith was being questioned, and handed me a visitor's badge to wear. A second cop appeared to take me.

"Are you coming?" I asked Sweeny.

"I'm sure she's in good hands," he said, and I last saw him heading toward the door. As I made my way through the labyrinth of the station, it seemed to me very likely that Sweeny had intentionally engineered Edith's visit here to assist the cop's intimidation of her. The man's duplicity appeared bottomless.

Edith was sitting beside a gray metal desk sipping coffee from a paper cup. My old friend, Detective Laverty, was at the desk, shirt-sleeves rolled and tie at half-mast. Merrill had his back against the wall. They looked up at me when I entered. I positioned myself behind Edith's chair.

Laverty acknowledged me with a bland, "Mr. Rios."

"Everything OK, Edith?" I asked.

She looked up at me, her face was impassive but her eyes were furious. "I'd like to go."

I looked at the detectives and said, "I see no reason why you shouldn't."

"Just a minute," Laverty said. "We believe Miss Rosen has material information about Senator Peña's death. We'd like her to cooperate."

"I told them that anything I know about Gus is protected by the therapist-patient privilege," she told me.

Laverty said, "This isn't about Peña, it's about one of her other clients, a kid named Michael Ruiz."

"The privilege would still apply," I said.

"This guy is a suspect in the Peña killing," Laverty said.

"You'll have to get your leads somewhere else," I replied.

Laverty droned, "We could hold her as a material witness."

"Detective, there is absolutely nothing in any statute in this state that allows the police to hold a citizen just because they think she knows something about a crime. So unless you have the proof to charge her with something, we're leaving."

"You ever hear of Penal Code section 148?" he asked.

"Resisting arrest?" I replied, "Please."

"It also covers obstructing a police investigation," he said.

"That's hardly the situation we have here. This woman is a psychotherapist. She has every right to refuse to answer any question that, in her judgment, violates the privilege. All you're doing is trying to bully her."

Merrill shifted his weight against the partition, and said, "She came down here on her own."

"So what?" I snapped. "You think this is sacred ground? You think the laws stop applying once you cross the threshold? Come on, Edith. let's go."

She stood up. "Thank you for the coffee," she told Merrill.

Laverty looked at her, then at me, and said, pleasantly, "Just follow the blue line along the floor. It'll take you out, and thank you for your time, Miss Rosen."

When we got outside, she took a couple of deep breaths and said, "Thank you, Henry, I was actually getting pretty nervous in there."

"Did you come with Chuck Sweeny?" I asked. When she nodded, I said, "He's gone. I'll give you a lift back to the house."

We started toward my car, which I'd parked in front of the federal building across the street from Parker Center. A couple of blocks away, lights blazed from the tower of City Hall. The smell of urine hung in the air. With the politicians and bureaucrats gone for the night, the homeless roamed the grounds of the government buildings looking for a safe place to bed down.

When we got to my car, I asked, "How do they know about Michael?"

"Chuck," she replied sourly. "You were right. They came back to the house and went straight to him. He must've told them that Michael had threatened Gus. Then they came to me and we ended up down here."

We got into the car. "Have you heard from Michael?"

"Not a word," she replied.

As I drove past City Hall, I said, "Now that they know about him, they'll be back, interviewing everyone at the house they think might know something. We've got to try to beat them to it."

"How?"

"Can you think of anyone at the house he might have confided in? Someone who might know where he is?"

She thought for a moment. "He had a roommate, a boy named Lonnie Davis. He was released from the house a couple of days ago. I'll find out where he's staying."

"Good. I'll talk to him." We drove on in silence for a few minutes. "Edith, I want you to forget about the privilege for a moment and tell me something. Why did Michael threaten Peña's life? Was there a particular incident?"

She hesitated.

"Look," I said, "I seem to be the kid's lawyer. Tell me so I can help him."

"It wasn't just a single incident and it wasn't just Michael who resented Gus. Henry, how much do you know about the house, about its rules, I mean?"

"Not much," I conceded.

"When you sign in," she said, "you agree to stay for three months. Your contact with the outside is strictly controlled. You have to participate in house meetings and group therapy. You're expected to observe curfews and submit to random drug tests. Everyone has to do it, but not Gus Peña. He stayed less than a month and he basically did whatever he wanted."

"Why did Gus get to bend the rules?"

"He was chairman of the senate committee that appropriates money to places like SafeHouse," she said. "Chuck wanted Peña to owe him a favor."

"I see."

"Michael didn't want to be at SafeHouse, and it really made him angry to see Gus flouting rules that he was forced to abide by."

"That still doesn't seem like enough provocation to want to kill someone," I said.

"No, it was Gus's arrogance that enraged Michael," she said. "The contempt with which he treated Michael. They really hated each other, and they fought with the kind of rage you only see in families."

▲

CHAPTER

ELEVEN

▼

LONNIE DAVIS LIVED IN A BIG PINK BUILDING IN WEST HOLLYWOOD
called the Essex House. The tatters of a garden clung to life in the
strip of dry earth between the sidewalk and the front wall. A faded
green awning sagged over the entrance. I dialed his number on the
security phone and a buzzer sounded. I pushed through the iron
door into the foyer. It led to a hallway where a picture window
framed a paved courtyard. In the center was a swimming pool surrounded by deck chairs. The last of the afternoon sun shone white
on the water. It was one of those secret moments when the city
reveals its true erotic nature; the light and the water like two skins
touching. I stood there in my too-warm suit, a breeze cooling the
uncovered surfaces of my body. The last thing I wanted to do was to
sit in a stranger's room either fencing with him or massaging his
memory. I would rather have tossed off my clothes and dived into
the water. Instead, I turned away and went down the hall looking
for Lonnie Davis's apartment.

Edith Rosen had called Davis a boy, so I had expected to find someone as young and uncertain as Michael Ruiz. The man at the door, wiry in Levis and a white tank top, was at least thirty. Years of hard living had dug furrows around his eyes and mouth, but his fine-boned face retained vestiges of once-innocent good looks. His blue eyes had the same stillness as the water outside, the same sexual depth. He looked at me as I had not been looked at in a long time.

"Lonnie? I'm Henry Rios."

"Come in," he said easily, stepping back.

He lived in a studio apartment, the big, square room unfurnished except for a mattress, a lamp and a portable TV on the floor at the foot of the bed. Two folded up chairs leaned against the wall. The bed was unmade. Balanced on a pile of paperbacks was an ashtray with a couple of cigarette butts in it. The blinds were drawn in the room's one window, but I could hear splashing in the pool outside.

He unfolded the chairs, planted them in the center of the room and said, "Have a seat. Can I get you a Coke or something?"

"That would be great."

He disappeared through a doorway, and a door squeaked open. I heard the jangle of ice and glasses. Among the books piled by the bed were the big book of AA, a book on meditation and *Swann's Way* with a bookmark stuck about a quarter of the way through.

He came back with two tumblers, saw where I was looking and said, "Textbooks to a new life."

"Does that include Proust?"

"Here, sit down," he said, and I heard a twang, something Southern in his voice. "I been carrying that book around for ten years," he continued. "You see how far I got. They tell me he's one of the great queer fathers."

The remark was an invitation for me to reveal myself.

"I tried reading him for that reason, too," I said, "but I didn't get as far as you did." I sipped my Coke. "You were Michael Ruiz's roommate at SafeHouse."

"Sure was. You mind if I smoke, Mr. Rios?"

"It's your house, Lonnie. Call me Henry, OK?"

He went over to the bed, picked up the ashtray and a pack of Merits, came back, lit one. "You want me to take your coat?"

I removed my coat and tossed it onto the bed. "That OK?"

"Yeah," he said, smiling. "It's good there."

"What about Michael, were you friends with him?"

He waved smoke away. "He was friendly enough at first but after I told him I was gay, he kept his distance. I guess he was afraid I would jump him."

"Was he afraid or was he hoping?"

"Mike was straight. I'm sure of it. Even before I told him about me he talked about a girlfriend."

"A girlfriend? Do you remember what her name was?"

He tapped ash into the ashtray which he had settled on the chair between his legs. "I don't remember right offhand. He only mentioned her a couple of times, after he called her. Like I said, that was in the beginning, before he knew about me. After that . . . " he shrugged.

"This is kind of important."

He ran stubby fingers through close-cut hair. "Let me think on it."

"Did he ever say anything to you about Gus Peña?"

"The senator? No. Is this about him getting killed?"

"Maybe," I said. "Was there anyone else in the house that Michael may have been close to?"

Lonnie smiled gamely, but shook his head, "Sorry, I know I'm not being much help."

"The girlfriend's name would help a lot, if you remember."

"Here," he said, rising from the chair. "Maybe I wrote it down." He walked across the room and opened the door to a closet. Back turned to me, he said, "I kept a journal while I was there. Coulda put her name in there."

He lifted his arms to a shelf, and I studied the muscles moving in his shoulders. The light in the room was changing, deepening. Shadows creased the jumbled sheets on the bed. I got up and went to the window, opening the blinds. Whoever had been swimming in the pool was gone, leaving wet footprints across the pavement and the water churning in its bed. Lonnie came and stood beside me. The notebook in his hands was filled with big, loopy writing.

"What are you looking at?" he asked.

"The water. You find anything?"

"Give me a minute." He bent his head over the book, slowly turning the pages. "Boy, was I fucked up," he said, and kept reading. "Hey, here it is. Her name was Angie." He pointed to a line in the book. I could make out the names Mike and Angie.

"Is there anything else about her?"

"Let me see. No, just that he said he called her that night." He closed the book. "Look, I wouldn't feel right giving this to you, but I'll finish reading it tonight, see if there's anything else in it about her."

"I'd appreciate it."

"Hey, you want to go swimming?"

I looked at him, ready to refuse.

"You really look like you need to cool off," he said. "I'll loan you a suit."

"OK," I said.

The water was as cool as I had imagined; the sky was blue and starless overhead. Lonnie had kept up with me for a couple of laps, then drifted over to the corner from where he watched me. When I'd had enough, I swam over to him.

"When you swim," he said, "you really swim."

"It feels good to use my body for a change."

"I know all about using my body," he answered. "That's how I ended up at SafeHouse."

"What do you mean?"

He hoisted himself up to the ledge of the pool, the water running streams down his thin, hard body. "I came out here from Tennessee to go to school, a long time ago. I was eighteen and pretty and there wasn't anything I wouldn't do in bed. I had a lot of friends." He pushed wet hair from his forehead. "Thing is, you don't stay young and pretty forever. It began to take more and more booze to keep up the illusion, not that anybody but me was fooled. The friends drifted off, the party moved on, and I woke up one morning and I was thirty-one, broke and a drunk." There was rue but no self-pity in any of this. "It was either pop a handful of pills or start over."

"You made the right choice," I told him.

"Some days that seems truer than others," he replied. "What about you? What's your story?"

I pulled myself out of the water and sat next to him, our legs touching. "Not that much different," I said, "except that when I woke up I was thirty-three, and a drunk, and I had a law degree."

"Well, if you studied the way you swim, I'm not surprised. You're not exactly laid back, are you, Henry?"

"No, not exactly."

The lights went on beneath the water. From an opened window above us came the sounds of TVs and radios and the aromas of food. Lonnie pressed his hand against the small of my back and asked, "You mind?"

"No, I don't mind."

Unfamiliar smells rose from the tumble of the unmade bed. The sheets twisted beneath him and his head sank into a pillow as I pushed into him. He grunted, pulled his legs tighter on my shoulders. I bent down as far as I could, the hairs of my chest glancing his smooth one. He lifted his head and kissed me roughly. With his free hand, he rubbed the tip of his cock against my stomach muscles. I raised myself up to keep from slipping out of him, and he jerked himself off, his warm come spilling across my skin. I stayed in him until I also came, then pulled out slowly. He grinned as he peeled off the rubber and dropped it beside the bed.

"Don't you wish old Jesse Helms could see us now?"

I grinned back. "No, not particularly." I flopped down on the bed beside him. "Of course, I'm old enough to remember when fucking a boy wasn't a political action."

"I haven't been a boy in a long time."

"But I bet you were a helluva boy when you were," I said.

He leaned into me, and I put my arm around him. "I guess we should clean up," he said, but neither one of us moved. The smells of chlorine and semen mingled in the air.

"Thank you," I said.

"My pleasure." He reached down for a towel and cleaned himself off, then handed it to me. "You have a lover, Henry?"

I finished with the towel and tossed it aside. "I think we're in the middle of splitting up. What about you?"

"I've never been the marrying kind."

"You want to go out and get something to eat?"

"Sure, after we take a shower."

After dinner I dropped Lonnie off at his place and drove home on Sunset. It was a beautiful night. I rolled down the windows, opened the sunroof, and a cool wind flooded through the car. At Sunset Plaza the sidewalk cafés were jammed with late night diners sitting in the glow of candlelight over pricey pasta dishes. Haute couture mannequins postured in the boutique windows. A woman in red leather walked a Great Dane while, behind her, the lights of the city blazed through the clear air. I was absurdly happy. For a couple of hours I had drifted on possibilities, something that had not happened in a long time, and it had been delicious.

When I got home there were four messages on the answering machine and the phone was ringing. Still buoyant, I answered it with a cheery, "Hello."

"It's Josh, Henry. I've been calling you for hours." His voice was edgy and frightened.

"What's wrong?"

"Steve had some kind of seizure. I'm at the hospital with him."

I sat down, uncertain of what to say. "Do they know what happened?"

"His doctor thinks it's toxo. They're waiting until tomorrow to do a CT scan. Right now he's sleeping."

"Which hospital are you at?"

"Midtown," he said. "I know this awkward, but could you come over, Henry, just for a little while?"

"That's over on Third and Genessee, right?"

"Yeah, I'll be waiting outside."

I left without playing the phone messages.

He was standing beneath a street light. I recognized the unruly hair and hooded red sweatshirt. I drove up to the curb and pushed the passenger door open. He scooted in, looked at me and said, "Thank you, Henry."

His hand was bandaged. "What happened?"

"I'll tell you later."

"Have you eaten?"

He shook his head. "Someplace close? I don't want to be away too long."

"I understand," I said, and started driving.

There was an all-night coffee shop not far away. Inside, bright lights bounced off orange vinyl and brown Formica. A chalkboard listed the homey specials: liver and onions, red snapper, spaghetti. Behind the counter was a display of pies and pastries. A bee-hived waitress led us to a booth and handed us oversized menus. Josh didn't even look at his, but told her, "Just coffee."

"Bring him the hamburger plate," I said. "I'll have iced tea and apple pie."

"All right," she drawled.

"I'm sorry if I was hysterical on the phone," Josh said.

"Tell me what happened."

The busboy brought our drinks. Josh measured milk and sugar into his coffee with his good hand. "When I went over to Steven's this afternoon he was in bed complaining of a headache. Um, I got into bed, too. I nodded off. The next thing I knew the bed was shaking like crazy. I thought it was an earthquake." He took a quick sip of coffee. "It was Steven, bouncing all over the bed. He sounded like he was choking. I didn't know what to do, so I sat on him to keep him from falling off the bed and pried open his mouth. He was swallowing his tongue." The coffee cup jerked in his hand and he set it down, the liquid spilling over the sides. "Sorry. I thought I was over it."

"It's all right," I said, covering his hand with mine. He grasped at my fingers. "You stuck your fingers in his mouth to keep him from swallowing his tongue."

He nodded. "He almost bit off my index finger, but eventually he stopped shaking, and was just sort of passed out. I called an ambulance. On the way to the hospital, he had another seizure. They took us both into emergency. They patched me up and I called his doctor. Then I started calling you."

The food came. The waitress set a big plate with a sloppy burger and heaps of french fries in front of him. He picked up the sandwich and bit into it greedily.

"It happened so fast there wasn't time to be afraid," he said, through a mouthful of food. He swallowed. "Afterwards, waiting to hear something, then I was afraid."

"I thought with toxo there were some warning signs," I said.

"Not always," he replied. "Sometimes a seizure is the first sign. That's the thing about this fucking disease. One day you're OK, and the next day you're in the hospital fighting something you didn't even know you had." He looked at the sandwich in his hand. "I don't know why I'm eating this. I'll probably throw it up later."

"Go ahead and eat. You'll feel better."

He smiled wanly. "You're always so practical, Henry. I bet you would've known what to do."

"If it's toxo, they can treat it, can't they?"

"Yeah, I guess." He began on his french fries. "They can treat it, they can't cure it. They can't cure any of it."

I picked at the apple pie while he ate. "I'm sorry, Josh," I said. "I hope he comes through it OK."

"This is really hard for you, isn't it?"

"What's hard is not knowing where we stand," I said.

"I can't come back," he said. "Everything is different now."

"You know you can always call me."

"Henry, I've known that since the first day I met you."

There was a fifth message on my machine when I got home that night. The first four were from Josh. The last one was a male voice saying, "Thanks for tonight."

TWELVE

THE NEXT DAY WAS THURSDAY, ONE WEEK FROM THE DAY THAT GUS Peña had been killed. The story had slipped from the front page of the first section of the *Times* to the front page of the Metro section. It had become as much about politics as it was about a murder investigation. One group of Latino leaders castigated the cops for not moving swiftly enough to find Peña's killer while another group deplored the continuing sweeps of the gangs in East Los Angeles. As far as the investigation itself went, a new phrase had slipped into the police communiques: a "potential suspect" had been identified. On my way into work, I dropped in at SafeHouse to talk to Edith Rosen. I found her at her cluttered desk, poring over the same story that I'd read at breakfast.

"I gather that Michael is their potential suspect," I said. "Any word?"

She folded the paper and set it down. "His parents have stopped talking to me," she said.

"Why?"

"After the police told them Michael had threatened Gus, his mother called and demanded to know why I hadn't told them sooner. I tried to explain that I couldn't, but she wasn't interested. She said if Michael's in trouble, I'm to blame."

"From what you told me earlier about them, I wouldn't have thought they'd care one way or the other."

"You'd have to meet her to understand," she replied. She lifted a mug from the corner of her desk and drank from it. "You want a cup?"

"No thanks. I want to finish our conversation about Michael and Gus."

"What do you mean?" She set the cup down on a folder.

"If it turns out that Michael did kill Gus, I want to know the chances of constructing some kind of psychological defense. You said they hated each other the way people in families can come to hate each other. What makes you think that?"

She rubbed her eyes wearily. By the looks of it, she hadn't had much sleep. "Do you really think it's going to help him?"

"I won't know until you tell me."

"You have to start with Gus," she said. "A self-made man who came up from a very hard childhood. His own father was an alcoholic and violent. Gus was the oldest son, so he took the brunt of it. You know he could've just as easily become a gang member himself and ended up with a criminal record and zero prospects."

"He was smart," I said. "That's what made him different."

She nodded absently. "Smart and angry. Even that's not always enough. To tell you the truth, Henry, I don't know what it is with someone like Gus. All the statistics were against him, but look what he made of himself."

I hazarded a guess from my own experience. "Maybe he looked around and saw what was possible. Maybe he imagined becoming someone."

"Yes, but how and when, that's the mystery. Wherever his ambition came from, it was ferocious. And unforgiving. Of him and others."

"This must be where Michael Ruiz comes in," I said.

"Michael had all the outward privileges that Gus never had," she said. "His family's well-off, and whatever else his parents may be, they aren't alcoholics. From Gus's point of view, Michael had squandered his advantages. Of course, Gus only knew half the story."

"What's the other half?"

We were interrupted by someone shouting in the hall, which ended as abruptly as it had begun, with the slamming of a door.

Edith said, "I think I already told you that Michael's parents were also strivers, like Gus, and just as successful. Michael paid the price for that."

"You told me he was basically raised by his grandmother."

"There's more to it than that," she said. "When he was three, he was rushed to the hospital with a concussion. His mother said he had fallen down the stairs. His father wasn't at home at the time. Child services investigated and he was eventually placed with his grandmother. Later, he was returned to his parents and the records were sealed. I only found out about it—," she stopped herself. "Well, it's not important. There is a record, and I found out about it."

"Did the abuse stop?"

"When I brought it up, Michael claimed he didn't know what I was talking about, but his behavior proves he was abused. If you tell a child he's bad long enough and often enough, he will act it out."

"'Those to whom evil are done, do evil in return,'" I quoted. "A line from a poem."

"The only evil Michael's ever done has been to himself," she said. "Anyway, you had Gus on the one hand playing the enraged father and Michael on the other playing the defiant son. And they were both Chicano, of course, which added that whole cultural element of standing your ground."

"I'm familiar with it," I said.

"I don't believe Michael killed Gus," she said. "I don't think he had it in him but, if he did, it came out of that struggle."

"We have to find him," I said.

"I know," she answered. "Why don't you try the parents. Maybe you'll have better luck than I did." She reached for her Rolodex and turned it to *R*, then searched for a card. She jotted down an address in the valley and a phone number. "His mother's name is Carolina and his father's called Bill."

I pocketed the slip of paper, thanked her, and left.

Although I left a couple of messages at the Ruizes' house, Carolina Ruiz didn't return my call until the next afternoon. I was at my desk dictating notes from a reporter's transcript of a murder trial into a hand-held tape recorder. Another dozen volumes of transcript sat on my desk waiting to be gone through. I had picked up this appeal from a colleague who had tried it, assuring me that the judge's errors would leap off the pages. So far, however, all the record had revealed was a bad case of judicial temperament. I was relieved when the phone buzzed.

"Carolina Ruiz," Emma said in the tone of voice she reserved for assholes.

"OK, thanks." I pushed the button to the outside line. "Mrs. Ruiz?"

She opened with, "Who the hell hired you as Michael's lawyer?"

I marked my place in the transcript and shut it. "The director of SafeHouse tried to kick Michael out. Edith Rosen asked me to talk to the man. We worked something out and Michael stayed. When it became clear that the police were looking for him in connection with Gus Peña's murder, Mrs. Rosen asked for my help again. No one's actually hired me."

"You're damn right," she said. "If Mikey needs a lawyer his father and I can take care of it."

"I think he needs a lawyer."

"He hasn't done a thing," she replied.

"Mrs. Ruiz, at minimum, he's in violation of his probation for leaving SafeHouse, and he's also a suspect in Gus Peña's murder. The moment the police find him, they'll put him on a probation hold and lock him up. That'll give them all the time they need to interrogate him."

She wasn't as quick to answer, but her tone was still rancid when she did. "My son didn't have anything to do with Gus Peña getting himself killed. If that woman hadn't talked to the police Mikey would still be at SafeHouse."

"Mrs. Rosen isn't the one who told the police about Michael's threat."

"Look, I don't care who said what to who. My son didn't do anything wrong, and he doesn't need you."

"All right, Mrs. Ruiz, have it your way. You're right, no one has hired me to represent Michael, so I'll back off, but take my advice and get your kid a lawyer. When the cops catch up to him, he's going to need all the help he can get."

"Don't tell me how to take care of my son," she said and hung up.

I put down the receiver and said to Emma, who had come in at the tail end of the conversation, "How would you like to call her mommy?"

"She's no mommy," Emma said, making a face. "That woman's a mother. You want to sign these checks?"

I signed the stack of checks she had put in front of me. "How did two nice people like us end up in this line of work?"

She shook her head, jangling her intricately braided hair. "I like to eat. You like to save the world."

"Not that the world has ever noticed."

"You just have those Friday P.M. blues, Henry," she said. "Take the rest of the day off."

"I'm looking for a needle in a haystack," I said, indicating the pile of transcripts.

"They ain't going nowhere."

"You know what? You're absolutely right. Take off, Emma, we're closed."

After she left, I sat in my office wondering what to do with the first free weekend I had given myself in months. The thought of going home to an empty house made me want to sleep on the couch in the lobby. I considered calling Lonnie Davis, but that kind of excitement wasn't exactly what I wanted either. Then I remembered Eric Andersen and his lover Andy Otero.

I had known Eric since college. He and Andy lived outside of Santa Barbara, on an avocado ranch that had been in Eric's family for eight generations. I saw him once or twice a year when he came into the city, and he had been urging me for years to come up and stay at the ranch. I dialed his number, already halfway up the coast in my imagination.

The ranch was deep in a canyon off the Coast Highway, accessible by a narrow rutted road that cut through bare brown hills and meadows shaded by great eucalyptus trees. Cows grazed peacefully along the road. Eric and Andy lived in a cottage that had been built by Eric's great-grandfather, a descendent of a Mexican land grant family, in the 1890s. The two men had lovingly reconstructed it.

They had been lovers for sixteen years, from the time that Eric had returned to Santa Barbara at twenty-four to take over the ranch. He met Andy, then an eighteen-year-old high school senior, who was working as a ranch hand that summer. Physically, they could not have been more dissimilar: Eric tall and blond, the son of a Mexican mother and a Danish father; and short, black-haired Andy Otero, one generation away from a Mexican village in Guanajuato. They loved each other and the ranch, and it was hard to tell where one left off and the other began. When he wasn't working the place, Andy painted.

In his landscapes, the golden earth rolled like waves beneath a mild, benevolent sky, bare but for wooden fences and clusters of oak and eucalyptus. In other scenes, the squat avocado trees hovered like green clouds above the dark loam. His paintings caught perfectly the silty quality of light, the dry yet fertile countryside. Although the ocean lay just over the ridge of the canyon, Andy seldom pictured it directly, but there was a quality to his landscapes in which it was always suggested, as if the land was like a shell washed up from the water. The smaller the subject of the painting, the more he implied. In a still life of avocados, one sliced open, the green and yellow flesh glistened with all the sensuality of the earth from which it had sprung.

I spent much of the weekend tramping through the ranch with one or both of them. It was good, particularly, to talk to Eric. He listened uncomplainingly while I went on for hours about Josh, acknowledging the loss to myself as I described it to him. And he understood when I talked about the confusion I felt over the direction my life had taken, because he remembered me as an eighteen-year-old boy in torn jeans and a black sweatshirt who had lived and breathed poetry.

On Sunday, while they went into town to mass—a rose window in the church commemorated one of Eric's ancestors, and Andy's parents still worshipped there—I took a paperback edition of W. H. Auden's poems and went up to the top of the canyon from where it was possible to see the ocean on one side and the ranch on the other. I sat on a boulder and turned the pages, encountering lines I had not read in fifteen years.

I stopped at a poem called "The Hidden Law" and read it over and over again. It was a short work, about the invisible rules that run our lives and which we, in turn, spend our lives running from.

The Hidden Law does not deny
Our laws of probability,
But takes the atom and the star
And human beings as they are
And answers nothing when we lie.
It is the only reason why

No government can codify
And legal definitions mar
        The Hidden Law.
Its utter patience will not try
To stop us if we want to die:
When we escape It in a car
When we forget It in a bar
These are the ways we're punished by
        The Hidden Law.

The words had the impact of a revelation, and although I didn't completely understand what it meant, I did know that it was an admonition to change my life.

▲

CHAPTER

THIRTEEN

▼

I LEFT SANTA BARBARA EARLY MONDAY MORNING AND DROVE DIRECTLY
to Raymond Reynolds's office in Beverly Hills for my eight o'clock
appointment. The tranquility I had felt at the ranch evaporated
somewhere between Oxnard and Rodeo Drive. By the time I spotted
the first Armani-clad studio executive in his BMW it was as if I had
never left town. I was relieved to step into Reynolds's quiet brain
cell of an office.

As I did, I again felt that there was something familiar about it
from my past; then it occurred to me: each time I entered his office,
I had the same sensation I'd felt when, as a boy, I entered the con-
fessional. It was that feeling that I was going to come clean. I sat
down on his squeaky couch and tried to make sense of my moment
at the ridge of the canyon.

"What kind of change in your life do you think you have to
make, Henry?" he asked me.

"I don't know," I said. "That wasn't part of what I felt up there. It
was more like a memory than a premonition."

"A memory of what?"

"A memory of what it felt like when I was eighteen," I told him. "The incredible sense of freedom at having finally got out from beneath my father's thumb, and how, for the first time in my life, I felt truly alive. There were so many choices, so much to experience, and I really believed that I could do it all. That lasted until he died. After that, the choices seemed to narrow. It wasn't that anyone said to me, 'The fun's over, decide what you're going to do for the rest of your life.' I just began to see things differently."

He rocked forward in his armchair. "How?"

"You know, Raymond, it was as if, once he died, the weight of his life descended on my shoulders and I—"

The phone rang. "My machine will take the call," he said.

I started to speak, but the phone rang again.

"I'm sorry, Henry, but I'd better take this." He answered the phone, listened for a moment, then said, "It's your secretary. She says it's urgent."

I got up and went over to his desk, taking the phone from him. "Yes, Emma."

"Henry, Mrs. Rosen called. The police have arrested Michael Ruiz. She's at SafeHouse and she says it's urgent that you go there right away."

"Call her back and tell her I'm on my way." I hung up and told Reynolds, "I'm sorry, Raymond, I have to go."

"What about freedom?" he asked gently.

"I'm really sorry."

Just as I pulled up at SafeHouse a TV station van was pulling away. Inside, there was a loud, crowded meeting being held in the dayroom. I made my way to Edith Rosen's office where I found her briskly cramming file folders into a floppy shoulder bag.

"Edith, what's going on?"

She stopped what she was doing. "I've been fired." Then she collapsed into her chair, muttering, "What a morning."

"What's going on out there?" I asked, pointing toward the day-room where someone was shouting invective at someone else.

"The house is meeting to talk about what happened this morning."

"What did happen this morning?" I asked, dropping into a chair.

"Michael turned up looking for me. He wanted to negotiate surrendering to the police. Unfortunately, I hadn't arrived yet. Before he could get away, Chuck saw him and had two of the staff hold him down physically while he called the police. Apparently, Michael struggled pretty loudly and roused the entire house. I got here just as the police were trying to get him out."

"Trying?" I asked. "Was he resisting?"

"It wasn't Michael as much as it was the other residents," she replied. "Most of them weren't aware that the police were looking for Michael as a suspect in Gus's murder. They didn't know why Chuck had called the police on him. All they saw was another resident being dragged off by a dozen cops."

"I see," I said. "I imagine Michael wasn't the only resident who'd had run-ins with the cops."

"It turned into a small riot," she said, wearily. "The police arrested three others as well as Michael."

From the dayroom, I heard Chuck Sweeny screaming for quiet, but his cries were drowned out by boos and catcalls. Someone skidded past the door sobbing. Unanswered, a phone rang and rang.

"It didn't help that the cops came in like an invading army," she said.

"What's this about being fired?"

"Chuck blamed me for everything," she said. "And told me to get my ass out of here." She managed a limp smile. "Under the circumstances, that doesn't seem like a bad idea."

"Does he have that authority?"

She looked at me raggedly. "Now is not the time to test it. Look," she continued, "this is really bad for the house, all of it. The fact that Chuck let Gus use the house as a front, Michael's arrest, the police. It's going to take a long time for SafeHouse to recover from this, if it ever does."

"What about Michael? Did you get a chance to talk to him?"

"No. I called you thinking you could get to him."

"I don't know, Edith. I talked to Carolina Ruiz, and she more or less fired me. I can't really hold myself out as his lawyer at this point."

She stood up. "You have to help him."

"Edith, there's a limit."

She grabbed the phone and started dialing.

"Who are you calling?"

"Carolina Ruiz," she said.

I took the phone from her. "Come on, Edith, right now, you need to calm down. Let's get out of here."

She started to reply, but then swept a couple more folders into her bag and said, "Buy me a cup of coffee."

I got her out of the house and we drove to a restaurant down the street. I sat her at a table, ordered coffee, and then went off to call Carolina Ruiz. The news of Michael's arrest broke through her hostility and she grudgingly agreed to allow me to find him, making sure I understood that I was not officially retained. I called around the police department until I found out where Michael was being held. I left instructions that he was not to be interviewed or moved until I arrived, then I returned to Edith.

"Michael's being held at the Beverly station," I told her. "I have the family's permission to keep the cops from beating a confession out of him."

She looked up at me gratefully. "You should go."

"In a moment," I said. "I could use some coffee myself." I flagged the waitress down. After she left, I said, "How do you know Michael wanted to turn himself in?"

"That's what he told the girl at the desk when he came in this morning."

I gulped some coffee, burning my tongue. "That's not good news."

Her face sank. "Oh, my God. You think he killed Gus?"

"That's the implication."

"What's going to happen to him?"

"Well," I said, "the cops will put him on a probation hold which will allow them to keep him until a hearing can be held. If they're going to charge him with Gus's murder, he has to be arraigned within forty-eight hours. In other words, they'll have plenty of time to talk to him."

"I really think you should go," she said.

"You'll be all right?"

"Yes, I'm fine."

"OK," I said, getting up. "I'll call you later."

The police station on Beverly was a squat concrete building, its gray facade completely unblemished in contrast with the surfaces of its neighbors, all of which were covered with gang *placasos*. Inside, it was blue walls and wooden benches. The grim visage of the current chief of police scowled at me from a photograph mounted on the wall. The counter was glassed in with bulletproof glass. The cop who was working it sauntered over to me and slid open a panel.

"My name is Rios," I said, laying my card on the counter. "You're holding my client, Michael Ruiz."

He studied the card, slid the panel shut, and stepped back toward a door. He opened it, shouted something I couldn't quite hear and a moment later, someone shouted something back. He returned to me, slid the panel open and said, "Gone downtown."

"I told your booking officer not to move him until I got here."

He gave me that you-asshole-can't-you-see-my-uniform look

that they were trained in at the Academy and said, "I said he's downtown."

I fumed, but said nothing, planning to take it out on the next cop I got on the stand.

At Parker Center, I was kept waiting twenty minutes until the officer on duty confirmed that Michael was there. It was another ten minutes before I was taken back to the interrogation room where I found him in the company of Detectives Laverty and Merrill. Michael had a black eye and his wrists were badly bruised. There was a strong smell of piss in the room and I looked at his pants and saw they were soaked. He looked terrified.

All my rage boiled over. "You people are fucking animals."

Laverty bridled. "Watch your mouth."

"You've got a lot of nerve," I said. "You beat my client, force him to sit here in his own piss, and you object to my manners." I took a step toward Laverty. He remained motionless, staring me down. "'To protect and serve,' isn't that what your badge says? Who do you protect? Who are you serving? Your testosterone?"

"I don't take that shit in court and I don't take it here," he said.

"What are you going to do, throw me out?"

His face reddened and he balled his hands into fists. I was dimly aware of Merrill moving against the far wall. Laverty threw him a sharp look, then said, in a tight voice, "You want to talk to your client, or what?"

"I'll talk to him. Alone."

After they left, I turned back to Michael, my pulse still racing from rage. He looked almost as afraid of me as he had of the cops.

"What did you tell them?"

"I didn't tell them nothing," he squeaked.

I sat down and drew a long breath. "Sorry," I said. "I'm a little worked up. Look, are you OK? I mean, is anything broken?"

"No, man. I'm OK."

"Good. I don't think either one of us is in any shape to talk right now. I'm going to have them take you to the jail ward at county hospital to have someone look you over and I'll come find you later. In the meantime, don't say a word to anyone about anything. And don't give them any excuse to hit you. You understand?"

"I understand," he mumbled.

"Good." I patted his arm. "Just do as I say and you'll be fine."

"You gonna leave now?" he asked in a scared voice.

"I'll be back in a few minutes. Just hold tight."

"Yeah," he said skeptically.

Laverty was out in the hall. I told him that I had to make a couple of calls, but would be back and to keep Michael there. Almost imperceptibly, he nodded. I found a pay phone and dialed a number that I had promised the man at the end never to use except in an extreme emergency.

"Chief's office," a male voice said.

"Let me speak to Captain O'dell."

"Who's calling?"

"Tell him it's Henry Rios."

"Hold."

When the chief of police had been asked why the LAPD refused to hire gay officers he sniffed, "Who would want to work with them?" unaware that he rubbed elbows daily with a gay man, a deeply-closeted captain in his own office. I had been introduced to Cliff O'dell by my friend Terry Ormes, the highest-ranking woman in the San Francisco police department, when O'dell and I had both been up in the city over a long weekend a couple of years earlier. Since then, he and I would have a discreet lunch somewhere. I had become the sounding board for all the frustrations he felt over his split life. I had never asked any favor in return, until now.

"Henry," he said gruffly. "This better be important."

"It is," I said. "You're holding a client of mine in an interrogation room on the fourth floor, room number 418. He's a suspect in Gus Peña's murder."

"I know all about it," he said. "We're preparing a press release. Jesus, how the hell did you get involved?"

"That's not important. Listen, he was man-handled by the arresting officers, and he's sitting up there in his own piss. I don't exactly trust the investigating officer to respect his constitutional rights."

There was a long, tense pause. "What do you want me to do about it?"

"I want him transferred to county hospital so a doctor can take a look at him, and I don't want him fucked with in the process."

"You must think we're Nazis," he said disbelievingly.

"Let's not get into that," I said. "All I want right now is for my client's rights to be respected."

"What's the officer's name?"

"Laverty, and there's another one, Merrill."

"Yeah, OK. Where are you calling from?"

"Downstairs, and I'm about to go back up. And Cliff, I want the murder book, and I don't want any trouble getting it."

"Don't ever call me here again," he said, and hung up.

When I returned upstairs, Laverty was still in the hall, talking to a good-looking man in a business suit who barely acknowledged me as I approached.

"Mr. Rios?" Cliff asked. "You the attorney?"

"Yeah, who are you?"

"Cliff O'dell, from the chief's office. Is Michael Ruiz your client?"

"That's right."

"I took a look at him," he said. "I think we need to get him checked out by a doctor."

"That's fine," I said. "I've instructed him not to answer any questions. I assume he won't be asked any."

"We're all aware of the exclusionary rule, counsel," he said sharply.

"I'd like the investigation reports."

O'dell glanced at Laverty. "Make copies for the man."

Laverty tightened his jaw. "Yeah, sure."

"We'll take your man down, now," O'dell said.

A few minutes later, Michael was being gently led to a waiting car to be taken to county hospital.

CHAPTER

FOURTEEN

▼

BACK IN MY OFFICE, I MADE A QUICK CALL TO CAROLINA RUIZ. THE
news about Michael's arrest had broken and the Ruizes were del-
uged by the press. I advised her to say nothing and told her to come
to my office with her husband at four that afternoon. Afterwards, I
phoned Edith Rosen and told her to come as well. Finally, I called
a friend to cover for me at a court appearance I had in Pasadena
after lunch, ordered a sandwich from a nearby deli, and settled in
to read the murder book I'd obtained from the cops. It included the
initial reports and follow-ups, witness statements, the autopsy, ballistics, and related reports.

The initial report contained a brief account of the crime scene
with photograph and diagrams. Peña had been shot in the parking
lot of a Mexican restaurant on First Street. The lot was behind the
restaurant, accessible from a side street by an alley. From a photograph, I made out a fenced lot reached by a staircase from the
restaurant's exit on the second floor of a brick building. The lot was
shadowy, illuminated only by porch lights on the landing of the

stairs and lights from the surrounding businesses. There was a big tree growing in the corner and a Dumpster pushed up against it. The lot was empty in the picture, but according to the report, there had been a number of cars in it when the shooting occurred. The police theorized from tire tracks in the alley that the killer had driven up, stopped in the alley beneath the tree, got out of the car, shot Peña, and then skidded out.

This was significant information. In a drive-by shooting, the shooter never gets out of the car. Under the cops' scenario, the shooter had actually been waiting for Peña or someone to come into the lot and had hidden himself while he waited. I turned to the autopsy report, my eye falling briefly on the diagram that showed where the bullets had hit. Gus had been shot five times; whoever had killed him wanted to be sure he was dead. All in all, the killing suggested a degree of planning and premeditation not usually associated with gang shootings.

I kept reading. Despite the gang sweeps in East LA, there had never been a serious suspect other than Michael Ruiz. Included in the book was Chuck Sweeny's statement, recounting Michael's threat on Gus's life, and his absence from SafeHouse the night of the murder. There was a list of people to be interviewed, including the Ruizes and Lonnie Davis. Also briefly noted was Edith Rosen's consistent refusal to discuss either Peña or Michael Ruiz. Still, the case against Michael had been weak until the police got a break, an eyewitness.

He had surfaced over the weekend, a young man named Pablo Saenz who had been working as a busboy at the restaurant the night Peña was killed. Just before the shooting, Saenz had come into the lot to empty some trash into the Dumpster. He had seen a big, beat-up car parked in the alley, and a man leaning against it. He couldn't make out the man's face clearly, but he could tell that he was Latino, about five-seven, thin, and dressed like a gangbanger. Saenz had been in the neighborhood long enough to recognize potential trouble, so he had quickly dumped the trash and started back to the restaurant.

At the foot of the stairs, he saw Peña coming down, and he stepped back to let him pass. He heard the man at the car call out Peña's name. Fearing violence, Saenz scooted into the shadows. From there, he saw Peña approach the man, and then heard the sound of a gun going off. He flattened himself against the ground and when the shooting stopped, he ran.

Saenz was an illegal, an immigrant from El Salvador. He had not come forward to the police because he was afraid that he would be deported. Eventually, the police tracked him down anyway and got his statement. From it, they prepared a photo lineup that included Michael's booking picture from his previous arrest. The result: a tentative make on Michael. I looked in vain for the photo lineup. Laverty had neglected to include it.

The tentative identification was the most damaging evidence but also the most fragile. Saenz had told the cops he hadn't gotten a clear look at the shooter. Despite that, he had identified Michael. It didn't take much imagination to guess at the pressure that had been brought to bear on the man. Faced with the prospect of deportation, Pablo Saenz would have been more susceptible than most witnesses to the suggestion that it was Michael he had seen. Burdened by the need to make a quick arrest, the cops would have been none-too-subtle in making the suggestion. Perry Mason notwithstanding, it's the rare case in which a defense lawyer can conclude that the police have arrested the wrong man. This was that case.

Carolina Ruiz was slender and well turned out in a silvery silk dress and blue blazer. Her short black hair was threaded with gray. I could imagine that she had once been lushly beautiful with her clear, dark skin and deep, probing eyes but now she seemed desiccated, drawn and hard-jawed. She sat at the edge of her chair lighting a cigarette. Her husband, Bill Ruiz, was barrel-chested and thick-waisted. His heavy, sweaty face registered worried amiability. He wore handmade Italian loafers, khakis, and a Ralph Lauren polo shirt, the little red horseman riding a plump breast. Edith had not yet arrived. I decided to start without her.

"Thank you for coming," I said. "I checked with the police a few minutes ago and Michael's been released from the county hospital and taken to county jail. I'll be talking to him in the morning."

"How is he?" she demanded.

"He has some bruises and a black eye, but other than that, he's fine. The police are claiming he was injured trying to resist arrest."

"What else would they say," she said scornfully.

"I've asked Edith Rosen to be here," I said.

"Why?" Carolina asked sharply.

"I thought she might have some insight into Michael's behavior."

"I can't stand that woman," Carolina said. "All she's done is teach Mikey to hate us. Everything was all right before she got her hands on him."

"Michael was on probation for armed robbery when he went to SafeHouse," I said.

"Armed robbery? He took a water gun into a grocery store and they called it armed robbery," she said.

"Mrs. Ruiz, your son has a serious drug problem."

She exhaled a thin line of smoke. "It's those punks he hangs out with at his grandma's."

Edith Rosen appeared at the doorway. "I'm sorry I'm late."

"Come in," I said. "We were just starting."

She crossed the room and sat on the sofa. Bill Ruiz smiled acknowledgment at her. Carolina Ruiz looked straight ahead.

"Let me tell you where things stand," I said. "Michael hasn't been formally charged yet, but I imagine the DA will allege first-degree murder. I don't know whether they'll be seeking the death penalty."

"The death penalty," Bill Ruiz said anxiously.

"It's entirely possible," I said, "but we won't know until the arraignment."

"Which is when?" Edith asked. Carolina Ruiz glared at her.

"They have to arraign him by Wednesday at the latest," I replied. "Of course, he'll plead not guilty. After that, there'll be a preliminary hearing. The purpose of the prelim is to determine whether there's enough evidence to support the charge. If the judge thinks there is, then the case will be set for trial."

"Is there enough?" Bill Ruiz asked.

"Yes," I said, "but it takes very little."

"What evidence?" Carolina snapped, crushing her cigarette in the ash tray.

"I'll come to that. At the trial, the DA has to prove that Michael's guilty beyond a reasonable doubt. That's a very heavy burden. Michael doesn't have to prove anything. He doesn't even have to testify."

Unable to restrain herself, Carolina broke in. "It's all lies. Mikey wouldn't hurt anyone. We knew Gus Peña, for God's sake."

I glanced at Edith who seemed as surprised as I was.

"Really?"

"My husband," she said, tugging at his arm. "He's an important man. He gave Peña money for his campaigns."

I looked at Bill Ruiz. "Did you know Gus well?"

He shrugged modestly. "Not to be friends," he said. "We went to a couple of fund-raisers for him when he was thinking about running for mayor. He came to our Christmas party last year. I talked to him once in a while. It was no big deal. When Mikey had his trouble, I called Gus to see if he could do anything for him."

"And?" I asked.

"He said jail would do him good."

"I see. Did you ever ask Gus for any other favors for Michael?"

"We tried to put him into the same school with Tino, Gus's boy.

A Catholic school. They didn't want to take him so I asked Gus to talk to the principal."

"Did it help?"

He nodded. "Mikey went for a semester," he spread his hands on his knees. "Then there was some trouble."

Carolina broke in. "You said there was evidence against Mikey. What evidence?"

"There was a witness to the shooting," I said. "He saw the man who killed Gus, not close up, but close enough to give the cops a description. The cops gave him a photo lineup with Michael's picture in it, and he identified Michael as the man he saw." She started to speak, but I cut her off. "He wasn't certain, and there wasn't anyone else around when the cops showed him the lineup. The witness is undocumented, from El Salvador."

"They threatened to send him back if he didn't say it was Mikey," Carolina surmised.

"There is that possibility," I replied. "As it is, there's an immigration hold on him."

"Would the police really do that?" Edith asked.

"Lady, you don't know the cops," Carolina said, addressing her directly for the first time. "I grew up in Boyle Heights. Those bastards have always had it in for Chicanos."

"I'm going to request a live lineup," I said. "One that I can monitor, to make sure it's conducted fairly. Then we'll see how things stand."

"Mikey didn't do anything," Carolina said, "and I don't care who says different."

"What I'd like to know," I said, "is where he's been for the past week. That doesn't look good at all."

"He was with his grandma," Carolina said.

I looked at her hard. "You told Edith he wasn't there."

"It was none of her business," she said.

"You realize he was in violation of probation," I told her.

She shrugged. "He was scared. He didn't trust the people at that place anymore." She glanced at Edith. "Can you blame him?"

From deep within his chair, Bill Ruiz asked, "What do you think, Henry?"

"About Michael killing Peña? I want to talk to him, of course, but except for the photo ID the evidence seems pretty weak to me."

"But do you think he did it?" Carolina asked.

"No," I said. "I don't."

Bill smiled. "Then you're our man, Henry."

"Unless you have other questions," I said, "that's all I've got for now."

They all sat there. Finally, Bill Ruiz bestirred himself and got up, his wife following reluctantly.

"Thank you," he said, and lumbered out, with Carolina behind him. She stopped at the doorway, glanced back suspiciously at Edith, then me, and left. I heard them arguing in Spanish on their way out.

"Mrs. Ruiz is a lioness," I told Edith. "I'm surprised. From what you'd told me about her, I would have expected indifference."

Edith said, "That's confusing guilt with love."

"Why do you say that?"

She came over to my desk. "I don't want to talk about Carolina. I want to talk about Michael."

"OK, what about him?"

"Well, actually," she said, taking the chair Carolina had been sitting in, "it's about you, too."

"Go on."

"You told them you don't think he killed Gus. Do you believe that?"

"This killing is beginning to look like it was carefully planned," I said. "Michael Ruiz is a punk, impulsive, short-sighted and self-destructive. I can't see him carrying it off."

She frowned. "You're supposed to be on his side."

"I'm supposed to defend him," I replied. "I don't have to like him."

"That's what I wanted to talk to you about. Don't write him off the way everyone else has."

"Meaning?"

"You're a lot like Gus, Henry, you know that? You pulled yourself up by your own bootstraps and you're not particularly tolerant of weakness in others."

I leaned back in my chair. "I don't think I'd be in this line of work if that were true."

"I'm not criticizing you," she said quickly, "just making an observation. Let's talk about Gus, then. Gus was idealistic, too. He believed that things could be changed, made better, and he believed that he could do it. After all, he had transformed his own life, hadn't he?"

"But."

"But not everyone is that strong," she said. "Don't be so quick to judge Michael. He has his story, same as you. He has his reasons, his motives, his aspirations. Maybe he can teach you something you need to know about this case."

"You know him better than any of us," I said. "What are his aspirations, Edith?"

"He wants to be loved," she said. "That's all he's ever wanted."

The tattooed teardrop trembled at the edge of Michael's eyes as he blinked at the harsh light in the interviewing room at county jail. He was pitifully thin in the blue jail jumpsuit and his face and wrists were still discolored with bruises. He didn't look as if he had slept much. I tried to keep in mind what Edith had told me the previous afternoon as I began our interview.

"How do you feel, Michael?"

"You got any cigarettes?" he asked in a raw voice.

I reached into my briefcase for the pack of Winstons I always carried for such occasions and pushed them toward him with a pack of matches. He tore at the wrapping and lit one with a shaky hand.

"Edith Rosen said you went to SafeHouse yesterday to turn yourself in. Is that true?"

"I wanted her to talk to the cops for me," he said, sucking at the cigarette. "See what kind of deal I could make."

"Deal for what?'

"If I copped to killing him."

I studied the boy across the table from me. I'd seen all kinds of killers, and couldn't rule him out just because he didn't fit the profile. "Did you kill him, Michael?"

"The cops said they got someone who saw me."

"That's not what I asked you."

He looked blankly around the room, smoking loudly.

"It's not a hard question, Michael," I said. "Did you kill him?"

"What kind of deal can you get me?" he rasped.

"I don't plead people who aren't guilty."

He looked at me coldly. "Yeah, I killed the asshole. You happy?"

"Tell me about it."

"I went down to the park and met up with some homeboys," he said, after a moment.

"Which park?" I asked, jotting notes on a legal pad.

"Griffith," he said. "There was some people there having a party. I got high, you know. Started talking shit to them about Peña. They're my people, man," he said, tapping his chest. "My enemies are their enemies."

"What happened next?" I deadpanned.

"One of them, Shorty, he's got a gun in his car, and he asks me, 'You want to go for a ride?' I said, 'Sure, let's go look for the asshole.' We drove over to his house."

"How did you know where he lived?" I asked.

"My dad knows him," he said. "He took me there a couple of times. He wanted me to meet his kid. Thought he would be a good influence on me," he added caustically. "We saw his car pulling out of the driveway, so we followed him. He went over to that restaurant."

"What did you do then?"

"Sat in the car and smoked some crack. Did a little wine. I got pretty fucked up. And we waited for him to come out."

"How long were you parked there?"

"Shit, I don't know. Couple of hours."

"Where did you park?"

"There's a big tree. We parked underneath it."

Exactly where the police had placed the shooter, I thought, making a note. "OK, then what?"

"Then I saw him coming out, and I got out of the car with the gun. I called him. He started coming over, and I guess I shot him. I jumped back into the car and we split. They dropped me off and I went back into the house."

"Did you see anyone else in the lot?"

"Some guy," he said, lighting another cigarette. "Looked like a waiter or something. He was dumping garbage."

For the next half-hour, I questioned him intensely about the details of the shooting. Every answer he gave was consistent with what the police had reported in their investigation. By the time we finished, I had little choice but to believe Michael Ruiz had murdered Gus Peña, but some part of me still doubted. I was still clinging to my original assessment of him as a punk dangerous only to himself; he lacked the metallic hardness I associated with murderers.

"You gotta get me a deal," he said again.

"If what you say is true," I told him, "then you haven't left me much room to deal in."

"You don't believe me?"

"I've sat in a lot of rooms with killers," I said. "You don't seem like a killer to me."

"Check it out," he said, laughing to himself. "My lawyer thinks I'm innocent."

I got up. "Yeah, it's funny all right, except that you may be going to prison for a long time."

His face darkened. "I ain't afraid of that."

"You think about that carefully, Michael. We'll talk tomorrow at the arraignment."

CHAPTER

FIFTEEN

▼

From the jail, I drove back to my office for a meeting with my investigator, Freeman Vidor. He was just getting out of his car, and I pulled up behind him. He stood on the sidewalk, watching a girl in a purple halter and matching pumps shimmy down Sunset waving at passing cars.

"I could use a little of that," he said, appreciatively.

I watched her sway toward the corner. "It's not like you'd have to ask her Dad's permission for a date."

On the way up to my office, he said, "You see the girls out here all day long. Don't you even get a little curious?"

"I satisfied my curiosity about girls when I was six years old and played doctor with Monica Parra. I saw what she had and I saw what I had, and I liked mine better."

He held open the door for me. "Six, huh? They get better when they grow up."

"I'll have to take your word on that."

"Hey, beautiful thing," he said to Emma as we passed her desk.

She lifted her hair from her computer. "Hey, yourself." To me, she said, "Josh called, said to tell you he would stop by the house tonight."

"Thanks. You want some coffee, Freeman?" I asked, ducking into the kitchen.

"Yeah, black and sweet as Emma."

"You are so full of shit," I heard Emma tell him as I poured the coffee, wondering why Josh was coming by. I hadn't seen him since the night Steven had gone into the hospital.

Freeman was in my office sitting on the couch, lighting a cigarette. I handed him his coffee and sat down next to him, opened my briefcase and got out my notes from my interview with Michael Ruiz.

"I see you got yourself another page-one case," he said.

"Yes, I saw the *Times* this morning."

Michael's arrest had made the front page. I had left Emma instructions to fend off the press until after the arraignment.

"So what you got?" Freeman asked, drawing lazily on his cigarette.

"A paradox," I said. "I have a client who wants to cop to a crime I don't think he committed." I related my interview with Michael.

"So, why don't you think he did it?"

I sipped some coffee, going over the reasons that had occurred to me as I had driven from the jail to the office. I was glad Freeman was there. He could test their plausibility for me.

"Let's start with the factual inconsistencies," I said. "First, Michael says there was gang involvement, but he doesn't belong to a gang. According to my source," I continued, thinking of Tomas Ochoa, "the Dogtown Locos don't want anything to do with him. Also, the cops have been sweeping the gangs for the past two weeks, since Peña was killed, and they haven't been able to turn up anything connecting the gangs to the murder."

"You trust your source?" Freeman asked.

"Not entirely," I admitted.

"Look, if some gangbanger was involved," he continued, "that don't mean the cops are going to find out about it. And didn't you tell me the other day about some *placas* with Peña's name in them?"

"That doesn't prove anything," I said.

"OK, what's your next point?"

"Michael says he waited for Peña a couple of hours out in the restaurant lot before the shooting. That's a long time. There must've been people coming and going, but no one's come forward to the cops and said anything about seeing a car out there."

"Like you said, Henry, it's only been two weeks. Someone could still turn up, 'specially now that there's been an arrest. The cops will put out the details and people will start remembering."

"Three," I continued, undeterred. "He said he was smoking crack and drinking but he managed to hold the gun steady long enough to blast Peña five times. As far as I can tell, Michael has no experience with firearms."

"That's thin," Freeman said. "All he had to do was point it."

"I just don't think he did it," I said.

"On those facts?"

"Look, Freeman, you take the investigation report and read it. This murder took guts and a cool head. Michael Ruiz is a drug addict, a loser. OK, maybe I can't come up with facts why he didn't do it, but I trust my instincts."

Freeman said, "You're good, Henry, and I'm not saying you're wrong, but why would a kid cop to something this serious?"

"He wants respect from the gangs," I said. "He wants to belong. His therapist says he wants to be loved. What could get him more respect than this? We both know there are gangs in the prisons, and if he goes down on this, he might be a hero. Particularly if he's protecting the real killer, who is a gang member."

"Man, he would have to be desperate," Freeman said.

"He is that," I said. "Look, I don't trust my source on the gang connection. Maybe you can do better. He says the guy who was with him was a Dogtown *vato* called Shorty. Can you find out about that?"

"Sure, I can ask around. Bound to be a lot of Shortys out there, though."

"This one would have been in Griffith Park two weeks ago."

He scribbled some notes in a pad. "Anything else?"

"Peña had a universal reputation as an asshole," I said. "See if he pissed anyone off in the days before he died. Someone who would know his movements. You might start with his staff."

"Sure, what about the family?"

"They were with him when he was killed," I said.

"You think you could get your kid a deal?" he asked.

"Not at this rate," I said. "If he was as high as he said he was, there might be some kind of voluntary intoxication defense. That might bring it down to second-degree, but I'd have to take it to a jury even for that. The only other thing I can think of is to try to shake the eyewitness ID by doing a live lineup."

"That's risky," Freeman said. "He could pick your kid out again."

"Well, that would at least end my doubts about his guilt."

After Freeman left, I began to think more about a voluntary intoxication defense. It was a technical defense that went to the intent necessary to prove first-degree murder. If the defendant was so intoxicated that it was impossible for him, basically, to have held a thought in his head long enough to act on it, it could be argued that he lacked the requisite mental state required for first-degree. Michael's long history of drug abuse combined with his use of crack and alcohol that night might be enough to at least make the argument. His word alone, however, would not be enough. I tried to think of who might have seen him that night, after the shooting. The name I came up with was Lonnie Davis, his roommate at SafeHouse.

I slipped through the security door at the Essex House on the tail wind of another resident who eyed me suspiciously but was too busy with grocery bags to give me any trouble. In the big picture window that looked out on the pool, I saw a lone sunbather sprawled out on a chaise lounge, his face framed by the wires of his Walkman and obscured by sunglasses. It was Lonnie. I stepped outside and watched him for a moment.

Late afternoon shadows washed the pink walls of the buildings. The pool was a sheet of glass. The other night had faded into memories of body parts, wrinkled sheets, and restless sleep, but seeing him there brought the heat back. He reached down for a can of Coke, raised his head to drink, and stopped. A slow smile inched across his face. A moment later, I stood over him.

Slowly, the headphones came out, and the glasses came off. He put the Coke down and moved his legs on the chaise to make room for me. The smells of suntan lotion, sweat, and chlorine came off his hard, brown body. The blue eyes were welcoming.

"How do," he said. "Nice to see you, Henry."

"You, too," I said. "How have you been?"

"Passable. You?" He wiped sweat from his face and dried his hand on his bathing suit, a white strip of nylon, his genitals loose beneath it.

"I'm good. I never thanked you for the other night."

"Is that why you came back?" he asked, picking up the Coke. He handed it to me. "You look hot."

I took it from him, our fingers brushing, and gulped the sweet, sticky liquid. I remember how happy I had felt driving home from here that night—had it really been only a week ago?

"I wish that was the reason," I said. "This is business."

"Mike?" he asked. "I read about him in the paper this morning. You his lawyer?"

"Yes," I said. "Can you answer a couple of questions for me?"

"I'll try," he said.

"The night he broke curfew, did you actually see him when he came in?"

"Just for a couple of minutes," he drawled. "I was in bed already, half-asleep. He stumbled around a bit, woke me up."

"Stumbled?" I seized on the word. "Did he seem drunk to you? Loaded?"

Lonnie grabbed the towel his head rested on and wiped himself down. "Could have been. I didn't say 'boo' to him. Just saw it was him and went back to sleep."

"But he could have been wasted?"

"Sure," he said, easily. "He coulda been. Why are you asking?"

"I just want to get a clear picture of what happened that night," I said. "Have the police talked to you yet?"

A look of alarm crossed his face. "No, why?"

"The night Michael broke curfew was the same night Gus Peña was killed. Now that Michael's been arrested, they'll be questioning everyone who may have seen him."

He smiled. "What should I tell them?"

"The truth," I said.

He dropped the smile. "This *is* business."

"You may have to testify at the trial," I told him.

"I guess it wouldn't look too good if I was sleeping with one of the lawyers, would it?"

"No, it wouldn't."

A blond girl in an electric-blue swimsuit came out of the building and dived in at the far end of the pool. We watched her for a moment.

"Will I be seeing you again?" he asked.

"In court, maybe," I replied.

He nodded. "Did you know I might be a witness when you were here the other night?"

"The other night I was trying to find Michael," I said. "I didn't know until this morning how things were going to be."

"Can I believe you?"

The girl was still splashing around in the pool. I reached over, pulled him toward me, and kissed him. Someone cleared her throat behind us. We didn't stop. Finally, I let go of him, and pulled back.

"From here on out," I said, "we'll have to play it by the book. That doesn't mean I won't be back when it's over, if that's what you want, too."

"I think you know what I want," he said. "I'll walk you out."

As we headed toward the door, he said, "Oh, remember you asked me about Mike's girlfriend? Angie? I think I saw her once, for a minute. I was out on the porch smoking, and I saw a car drive up and Michael got out. There was a girl driving it. Pretty girl. He kissed her."

Remembering the car described at the site of the murder, I asked, "Was it old, beat up?"

"Hardly," he said. "It looked brand-new, one of those little Japanese numbers. Miata?"

I opened the door. "And the girl, did she go with the car?"

"Definitely," he said.

"See you in court, Mr. Davis."

"And I'll see you back here afterwards, counsel."

When I got home that night, Josh's car was in the driveway, the back seat packed with boxes. I walked into the house and found him bent at the oven. A thick steak lay in a pan of dark marinade. Water boiled in a pot on the stove, and asparagus lay drying on paper towels.

"Josh?"

He closed the oven door and turned around. "Hi, I'm making you dinner."

"I can see that," I said, laying my briefcase on the kitchen table. "How's Steven?"

Josh said, "I brought him home today." He poured himself a glass of wine from a bottle on the counter. "Can I get you something to drink?"

"No, thanks." It was strange to see him there, and then I thought of the clothes in the car, Steven going home. It all fell into place. "I saw your car out there," I said.

"I'd planned to be done before you got home, and just leave you a note, but that didn't seem right."

"Is this the last supper?"

He frowned, set his glass down.

"Sorry," I said. "Bad joke. I don't know what else to say."

"When I was moving stuff out, I looked in the fridge for something to drink," he said. "It was empty. I thought I'd make you something to eat, that's all."

"I'm not very hungry." I sniffed something burning. "Turn the broiler off before it sets off the smoke alarm."

He went over and shut the oven off, turned the flame off beneath the saucepan, then came and sat down at the table.

"I didn't know another way to do this," he said.

"You don't have to apologize," I said. "It's been coming for a long time."

"I'll always love you, Henry."

"Don't cry, Josh."

He wiped his face on his shirtsleeve. "I just couldn't keep pretending I was going to come back."

"It's all right," I said, stroking his face. It was an effort to talk, and all I really wanted was for him to leave. "How are you feeling? Your health, I mean."

"I'm down to ten T-cells. Doc's taking me off everything. AZT. DDI. The whole alphabet. I'm going to see an herbalist tomorrow."

"A what?"

"An herbalist," he repeated, defensively. "A specialist in Chinese herbal medicine. Steven swears by him."

"Steven just got out of the hospital," I pointed out.

"He's also lived five times longer than his doctors expected him to when he was diagnosed." His voice was beginning to show his temper. "What's it going to hurt, Henry? What have I got to lose?"

I didn't have an answer for that one. I never did. "Just be careful. Check out what he says with your doctor."

"Sure," he said without meaning it. I let it go.

"Leave me your phone number, OK, for mail, messages, that kind of stuff."

"It's on your desk." He dug into his pocket and took out a key. "The house key."

"Are you sure?"

He nodded. "Are you sure I can't feed you?"

"Not tonight," I said. I eyed the bottle of Bordeaux on the counter. "But take the wine, would you?"

He went over to the counter, picked it up and emptied it into the sink. He rinsed the bottle and dropped it into the recycling bin, one of his projects that I would now have to take on as my own. I watched him, graceful as ever, short and slender, moving through a room that had always been more his than mine. When he came back to me, I saw the terrible sadness in his eyes, and had to look away, at a blue bowl that he had filled with oranges. A small elegance. Josh had an elegant soul.

"The real reason I stuck around and waited for you," he said, "is, I wondered if we could make love."

"That's not necessary, Joshua."

"It's not what you think," he said. "It's not a favor to you. It's for me, if you'll do it. I was going to feed you by candlelight and then ask, but . . . " He smiled, wanly. "I'll go if you don't want me."

I reached out and pulled him toward me, pressing my face against his stomach, feeling his fingers in my hair, kneading my shoulders. After a moment, I got to my feet, and we went into the bedroom.

I tried to see everything as clearly as I could while we made love, but I was present only in the details: a sinewy, hairy thigh, the musk of his groin and armpit, the smooth expanse of his back. I ran my tongue across his teeth and touched the place where he had chipped a tooth years earlier, on a piece of hard bread at a restaurant in Carmel. For a second, I saw him wading into the ocean while I shot pictures from the shore. I held him close, his breath fluttering on my cheek. He whimpered softly as he came, and lay his head against my shoulder. Within minutes, he was asleep and then I slept, too.

▲

CHAPTER

SIXTEEN

▼

"I'm sorry I had to run off the other day," I told Raymond Reynolds the next morning. "If you've seen the papers, I guess you know what it was about." Michael Ruiz was scheduled to be arraigned at ten. Reynolds had agreed to see me at a very early hour. For once, the blinds on the windows were open, revealing a prosaic scene of telephone wires, a supermarket sign, a slate gray sky.

"Do you think it's significant that you left here because someone else needed you?" he asked.

"I'm on call pretty much twenty-four hours a day," I answered.

"Even the one hour a week you set aside for yourself," he observed. As always, his tone was mild, inquisitive, like a voice that questioned from within.

"I think I told you that I'm not the contemplative type."

"No," he said, "what you told me is that you didn't think the purpose of life is to sit beneath a tree and wait for enlightenment. It's a false dichotomy, Henry. It's not either-or. Just before you left last time, you were telling me how things changed for you after your father died. Is that when you decided to become a lawyer?"

"Not immediately," I said. "I drifted into it over the course of a couple of years. It was the tail end of the sixties, and I got caught up in the peace movement, or what was left of it." I thought back to those far-off days, and how, gradually, I had exchanged my books of Yeats and Auden for Herbert Marcuse and Frantz Fanon. "I became very grim, weighed down by the world's injustices."

"The world's injustice, Henry, or your father's?"

"I didn't have you around to make that distinction for me," I replied.

He smiled at my annoyance. "I doubt whether you would have heard it anyway."

"Well, anyway," I continued, "I could see that street protest was a dead end, so I looked around for another way to change the world. I came to law. Criminal law. I never considered any other kind of practice."

"And have you changed the world?"

"You know as well as I do the answer to that," I said irritably.

Undeterred by my tone, he asked, "So why do you persist?"

I ran through a list of responses in my head, but none of them seemed particularly persuasive. I said, "I feel like I have to justify myself to you."

"No," he said, "I don't care if you practice law or not. I'm just asking you a question about it you've never asked yourself."

"I have asked myself," I told him. "More in the last couple of weeks since Josh moved out than in the fifteen years that preceded it. The truth is, I don't know why I practice law anymore. I just can't imagine not being a lawyer."

"What do you think your father would think of your life, Henry, if he were alive? Do you think he would approve?"

"My father never approved of anything I did."

"Then what does it matter what you do?"

"That doesn't follow," I said.

"A few minutes ago you described yourself as grim and weighed down. Last time, you said when your father died it was as if the weight of his life had descended on your shoulders. But you also said that between the time you went away to college and his death, you felt free. What do those statements indicate to you?"

"Are you suggesting that I've become my father?"

"It's not so simple," Reynolds replied. "Just say you've become someone other than who you may actually be."

"I can't accept that. It would mean the last twenty years have been a waste."

"You've done commendable things in the last twenty years," he replied. "That's hardly a waste. They've all been for other people. What can you do for yourself?"

"That sounds so self-indulgent."

"If a man is tired and he rests, you wouldn't call that self-indulgent," Reynolds replied.

"Tired," I repeated. "You're right about that."

"*People versus Ruiz*," the clerk said. I moved forward from the gallery to the counsel's table, while in the jury box a bailiff nudged Michael who slowly got to his feet. He looked bad today, unshaven and red-eyed. I nodded at him. On the bench, Judge O'Conner turned irritably to his clerk and said, "I don't have the paperwork on him."

"It's here, Your Honor," she replied, handing him a manila folder.

He grabbed it from her then peered out past me to the television cameras at the back of the court. This was a high-profile case. Judge O'Conner was new to the bench, having last worked as a research attorney to an appellate court judge, and he was not enjoying his moment in the limelight.

He wagged a finger and said, "I want you people in the media to keep the disturbance down back there. This isn't 'LA Law.'"

While he busied himself with the file I glanced back at the

gallery. Bill and Carolina Ruiz sat toward the back. Edith Rosen was also there, but in another row. Behind the prosecutor's table was the Peña family; mother, daughter, son. Sitting beside the son was a tightly dressed blond whose bright lipstick gleamed like a headlight. Though she looked at least a decade his senior, she leaned into Peña's son with a proprietary air, and played with his fingers. Mrs. Peña glanced over, her face reproving. The daughter sat at rigid attention, looking at something in the corner. I followed her glance and saw that she was staring at Michael.

"OK," Judge O'Conner said. "*People versus Ruiz.* Let the record reflect that the defendant is in court. Is he represented?"

"Yes, Your Honor," I said. "Henry Rios for the defendant."

O'Conner smiled briefly at me. We'd been law school classmates and had lunch together whenever my work took me down to the court of appeal.

"Good morning, Mr. Rios," he said. "The People are also repre-sented by Ms. Castle—"

"No, Your Honor," a male voice boomed out from behind me. I glanced over my shoulder and saw Deputy District Attorney Anton Pisano stride importantly up the aisle. This was bad news. Tony Pisano was not only smart and tenacious, but an ambitious head-line-grabber with political aspirations. Having him in the other cor-ner would mean that everything would be played out in front of the cameras in hand-to-hand combat. I looked up at Alex O'Conner. His face was already turning an anticipatory shade of red.

"Anton Pisano for the People," Pisano said.

"Duly noted," O'Conner said sourly.

Pisano said good-naturedly, "You needn't sound so happy, Your Honor."

O'Conner replied, "We can dispense with the asides, counsel. Mr. Rios, does your client waive a reading of the information?"

"Yes," I said, moving away from the podium so that I could stand beside Michael.

"Fine. Michael Andrew Ruiz, you are charged with one count of violation of Penal Code section 187, murder in the first degree. How do you plead?"

"Not guilty," I whispered to him.

"Not guilty," he echoed wanly.

"Furthermore, it is alleged that in the commission of this offense you used a firearm within the meaning of Penal Code section 12022. Do you admit or deny this allegation?"

"Deny," I whispered.

"I deny it," he said, a little more fervently.

Before I could say another word, Anton Pisano was on his feet, talking. "Your Honor, anticipating a defense request for bail, the People would like to be heard."

O'Conner said, "Mr. Pisano, if the defense asks for bail, you will get a chance to respond." He looked at me. "Well, Mr. Rios?"

"The defense does request bail."

"Any particular amount?" O'Conner asked.

"The defense feels that bail in the amount of $100,000 would be appropriate."

There was no bail schedule for a capital offense, but $100,000 was the equivalent of offering $10,000 on a Rolls-Royce. While I didn't expect he would grant it, I thought I could at least pick the ballpark we'd be playing in.

Tony Pisano all but snickered, "That's ridiculous. Your Honor, this is first-degree murder, not," he paused to think of some sufficiently caustic comparison, "not expectoration in public."

I said, "From my experience, the Los Angeles District Attorney's office is quite capable of inflating spitting on a sidewalk to a capital offense."

"This defendant spits bullets," Pisano replied.

"Gentlemen," O'Conner said, irritably, "I don't find this exchange as amusing as you do. Moreover, I have a very long calendar this morning, and if this is going to be a dogfight, I'll never get through it. I'll set a bail hearing for three o'clock this afternoon. You want your client here, Mr. Rios?"

"Please. And, Your Honor, the defense would like the court to study the police report in this case."

"OK. The matter is put over until three o'clock. Let me call the next case."

I whispered to Michael, "I'll come back to lockup in a bit. Your parents want to see you. You OK?"

"Yeah," he said unconvincingly as the bailiff clamped his shoulder and said, "Let's go, Mike."

"Let's go outside," I whispered to the Ruizes. We stepped out of the courtroom, reaching the doors at the same time as Mrs. Peña, her children a step behind. There was a small anteroom between the court and the corridor, where lawyers harangued their clients and cut deals with each other. The seven of us entered it at the same time. Mrs. Peña walked quickly toward the door leading out, but Carolina Ruiz laid a restraining hand on the sleeve of her lilac suit jacket.

"Grace, you know my boy didn't have anything to do with this," she said urgently.

Graciela Peña shook off the other woman's hand. "I can't talk to you."

"Tino? Angela?" Carolina wailed as the children brushed by her. "My God, you know my son."

Tino stopped, the sleek blond hovering behind him, looking put out. "My mother is very upset, Mrs. Ruiz," he said, taking her hands in his. "I'm very sorry for your misfortune. Now the court must decide."

"Thank you, Tino," she whispered. Bill came up behind her and put his arm around her shoulder.

"There's a small conference room at the end of the hall," I said. We stepped out to the corridor. Icily coiffed TV reporters descended on us, microphones thrust out like harpoons.

"Do you have a statement?" one of them shouted.

"You've already heard our statement," I said. "'Not guilty.'" I hurried them down the corridor. The reporters might have pursued had Anton Pisano not also come out of the court, only too willing to have his picture taken.

Carolina Ruiz slumped down in a chair and dug through her purse for a pack of long, thin cigarettes. Her husband lit it for her, then settled back himself, looking miserable in his nice gray suit. I leaned against the wall. This room held some history for me. Once before I had brought the parents of a client accused of murder in here, and almost ended up in a fistfight with the father. I didn't think I'd have that problem with Bill Ruiz. I had the distinct impression that he was more puzzled than angry with Michael, as he might be with an investment that had inexplicably failed to pay off. Carolina was another story, entirely.

"Why didn't the judge give Mikey bail?" she demanded.

"He wants time to hear our arguments and think about it," I said. "We have a problem with the DA. Pisano's out to make a name for himself on this case which means he'll go to the mat on every issue. He'll try to get the court to set a prohibitively high bail. The good news is that the judge is fair."

Carolina tapped an expensively shod toe. "What does that mean, fair? He's an Anglo, isn't he?"

It was interesting to me how deeply embittered Carolina Ruiz remained about the Anglo world, even after all these years of living in it. Her husband, on the other hand, was thoroughly assimilated, even down to the Anglo diminutive he went by, Bill, while she remained defiantly Carolina—not Carol or even Caroline. I wondered what Michael made out of this mixed message about his ethnicity, and if it had contributed to his feeling of being an outsider.

"Technically, the only factors the judge is supposed to consider in setting bail is whether the defendant poses a threat to the community and the likelihood that he may take flight," I told her. "Unofficially, he may consider the defendant's past record, the severity of the crime, and so on. The reason I asked him to read the police report is to give him an idea of how weak the evidence is. I'm hoping he'll see that because this is a highly political case the cops needed to break in a hurry, they pulled Michael in as the first likely suspect. Maybe then he'll give us a break on bail." I paused, and considered my words carefully, not wanting to further inflame Carolina's suspicions. "Of course, he also knows this is the kind of case that people remember. If he releases Michael, and Michael skips, it would look very bad for Alex."

"Alex?" Bill asked.

"The judge," I replied. "We went to law school together."

"Good," Bill said. Connections was something he understood.

Carolina dropped her cigarette to the floor and crushed it with unladylike intensity. "I can't believe that bitch wouldn't talk to me."

"Mrs. Peña?"

"She should care that the bastard's dead?" she went on angrily. "He two-timed her with every woman who would have him."

"Who was the blond with them?"

She shrugged. "Tino's girlfriend, it looked like."

"She seemed a little old for him," I observed.

"Can we see Mikey, now?"

"Sure, but the reporters might still be out there."

"Screw them," she said, rising and smoothing her dress.

"Wait," Bill said, holding out a restraining hand to her. To me he said, "The bail, if it's more than $100,000 . . . "

"We'll put up the house," she snapped at him. "The apartment building. We have it."

"That's our retirement," he told her.

"How much is Mikey's freedom worth?" she demanded.

The argument was unwinnable, and he let it go. I watched her and wondered at the price of guilt.

"Let's go," I said, and opened the door. A pack of reporters headed toward us.

"Are you his parents?" someone shouted.

The Ruizes stopped, and Carolina said, "Yes, we're his parents, and we know our boy is innocent of this terrible crime."

I hurried them into lockup before any further questions could be asked.

I hung back against the wall while the Ruizes talked to Michael through a metal screen in one of four small carrels. The other three were occupied by lawyers talking to their clients. One of them glanced over his shoulder at me and winked.

"A hundred thou for first-degree," he said. "You're dreaming."

Michael sat facing his mother, his face expressionless. Once or twice he shook his head angrily. I heard her raise her voice, and Michael looked as if he were about to walk away, but then his father muttered something and Carolina spoke more softly. They looked a lot alike, Michael and his mother. Same coloring, same thin-faced intensity. It was as if they were each looking into a mirror, and not liking what they saw there. I wondered if one of them would learn to simply walk away.

I went up and said, "I'll leave you alone now. Michael, I'll talk to you this afternoon, before the bail hearing."

Out in the hall, the camera crews and reporters were gone and it was filled instead with the usual anxious men and women and jittery children. I was on my way to get a cup of coffee when I was intercepted by Edith Rosen.

"Do you think the judge will give him bail, Henry?"

"I'm going for coffee," I replied. "Come with me."

Downstairs, in the bleak cafeteria, a crazy woman sat at a table carrying on an animated conversation with someone who wasn't there. A hung-over lawyer downed an immense breakfast of fried eggs, bacon, potatoes and refried beans. I paid for our coffee and joined Edith at a table by the window that looked out on Temple Street. It was hot and gray outside; only mid-May, but the summer had already set in.

"I don't know whether he'll grant bail. The problem's not

Michael's criminal record, it's his habit of skipping out of places he's been put into by the court."

"I have an idea," she said, blowing on her coffee. "Have you heard of home surveillance?"

"I've read about it," I said, remembering an article in one of the bar association magazines, "but it's only used in misdemeanors."

"Drunk driving cases," she said, "to relieve overcrowding in the jails. People serve their time at home." She sipped her coffee. "They wear electronic ankle straps that send signals to monitoring devices in their houses that are connected to the probation office. We've had people at SafeHouse who wore them," she continued. "If they leave the house, a signal goes off and the probation office calls. If they don't get an immediate response, they send the sheriffs."

"I might be able to sell this to O'Conner," I said. "It's worth a try. What's going on with your job status at the house?"

"I'm not going to fight it," she said. "The reason I came downtown was to tell you that, and to tell you that I'm backing off from Michael's case. I've done everything I could for him."

"You've done more than that."

"I've done things I shouldn't have," she said. "I don't want to compromise myself further. I'm leaving him in your hands, now, Henry."

We sat and drank our coffee. I watched Edith, her kind face tired and drawn. I didn't have the heart to tell her that Michael had confessed to me. I hadn't told anyone, because I wasn't certain yet what to do with his confession.

The crazy woman got up and shook hands with the air. Edith watched her, then turned back to me, "Michael didn't look very good."

"A couple of nights in county jail will do that to you."

"I saw Mrs. Peña in the courtroom."

"Pisano likes to have the victim's family near at hand," I said.

"Attractive woman," she said. "Good-looking kids."

"Tino seems to have hooked himself up with a live one," I said. "The blond in the gold lamé halter."

"I noticed the mother didn't approve," Edith replied. "The girl seems very sweet."

"Yes, Angela." I had my coffee halfway to my mouth when I said this, and then a picture flashed through my head of Angela looking at Michael. Angela. "Angie?"

"What?" Edith asked.

"The girl's name. Angela. Angie. Edith, have you ever seen that girl around SafeHouse?"

She put her cup down. "She and her brother used to pick Gus up sometimes. He couldn't drive. His license was suspended."

"Did you ever see her talking to Michael?"

"No, as far as I know, they never met."

"They must have, though," I said. "Michael said he'd been to the Peña's house with his father, and he went to school with the son. Edith, do you remember what kind of car Angela Peña drove?"

"Oh, Henry, I don't notice things like that."

"Please, try to remember."

She pursed her lips thoughtfully. "It could have been, something like a sports car. It was small. White, I think."

SEVENTEEN

AFTER LUNCH, I WENT BACK INTO LOCKUP. MICHAEL WAS SITTING BY himself in a holding cell smoking a cigarette. His hand shook badly as he raised the cigarette to his mouth. After watching him for a moment, I realized the shaking wasn't the result of nerves; he was detoxing. At county, he was locked up in high power, away from the rest of the population, eliminating any chance for him to get in on the drug traffic that ran rampant in the jail house. He'd been completely clean now for almost four days. No wonder he was hurting.

The bailiff let me into the cell. "How are you doing?" I asked him.

He looked at me blankly, then said, "When is this going to be over?"

"Which part?"

"Everything."

I sat down beside him on the metal bench. "That's up to you, Michael."

"I don't know what you're talking about," he whined.

"Why don't you tell me about Angela Peña."

"I hardly know her."

"Michael, you were seen with her," I told him. "She dropped you off at the house in her little white sports car. You kissed her. I saw the way she looked at you this morning."

"Bullshit, bullshit," he muttered, but his head quaked. I touched his face. It was ice cold. He jerked away from me. "Don't fucking touch me."

"I'm going to have them take you back to county hospital."

"This isn't shit," he said. "I been through a lot worse."

"What about Angela?"

"What about her?" he said, slumping against the wall. "She's not my girlfriend."

"But you know her," I said.

He nodded. "She came to a party my dad gave," he said. "My mom made me go to talk to her. She's all right." He came back to the bench. "She came to SafeHouse to pick her dad up one day and we talked. That's all."

"The ride? The kiss?"

"She saw me walking and she gave me a ride. You think a bitch like that would let me touch her?"

"Lonnie Davis told me you talked to her on the phone," I said. "You told him she was your girlfriend."

He snickered. "I just told him that so he'd keep his hands off of me, that faggot. You're crazy if you think she wants me."

"Did you want her?"

"All I want is to get high," he said. "That's my sex."

"You sticking to your story about shooting Peña?"

"You want me to lie?"

"Why would you want to kill Gus Peña? He was practically a stranger to you. Did he find out about you and his daughter?"

"Fuck you," he said.

"I'm going to try to get you out on bail, Michael," I said. "There will be some pretty strict conditions. You'll be confined to your parents' house." I explained the home surveillance program. "No drugs, no alcohol. If the court goes for it, it's going to cost your parents a lot."

"Can't I stay with my grandma?" he asked, in a little-boy whine.

"I don't want you back in that neighborhood."

"You might as well leave me in jail," he said angrily.

"You might get your wish yet," I told him.

I got to court a few minutes before three and went over to the clerk. I requested a meeting with O'Conner in chambers as soon as Pisano arrived. She went back and returned a couple of minutes later to tell me the judge would see us. Pisano showed up with Tino Peña in tow.

"I've asked the judge to see us in chambers," I told him, when he got to counsel table.

His black eyebrows darted upward suspiciously. "About what?"

"He's expecting us," I replied, and headed back, Pisano hurrying to catch up.

O'Conner sat behind his desk in shirtsleeves, a half-eaten banana at his elbow, papers covering his desk. Having seen how uncomfortable he had been that morning, I was gambling that he would let us argue bail here, out of the public eye, make a disposition and present it as a fait accompli on the record. Otherwise, there was a good chance that the presence of the press would make him skittish, and I was afraid he would deny bail just to get the matter out of his court.

As soon as we sat down, I started, "Your Honor, the defense has a bail proposal that I wanted to run by you here instead of out there in that zoo."

"Wait a minute," Pisano broke in. "I want this on the record."

"We can go on the record at any point," I said. "But I'd like you to hear me out."

O'Conner rubbed his chin. Beyond him, a picture window

looked out on the *Los Angeles Times* building, looming like a mausoleum in the smoggy heat. "Well," he said, "as long as you're here."

"I object to this procedure," Pisano said, slapping his hand on the edge of O'Conner's desk.

O'Conner said, with great delicacy, "Mr. Pisano, don't damage the furniture."

"Why are we having this secret hearing?" Pisano insisted.

The judge frowned. "I don't like the implications of that," he said. "There's absolutely nothing improper in my discussing this matter with you in chambers."

"The cameras will still be there, Tony," I put in. "You'll get your chance to make your speech."

He glared at me. "Are you accusing me of impropriety?"

"Oh, please," O'Conner said. "Let's just get on with it. What's your proposal, Mr. Rios?"

"Over lunch," I said, "I did some research on a program run by the probation office called home surveillance." I explained the details. O'Conner seemed intrigued. "If you were to grant bail in this case, my client would be willing to accept home surveillance. That way, any concerns the court might have about risk of flight would be satisfied. Not," I added, "that my client poses any such risk. It's just that, understanding this is a high-publicity case, I thought the court would be more comfortable with releasing him under these conditions."

Pisano said, "If your client weren't such a bad risk, you wouldn't have had to resort to home surveillance. And anyway, there's the public safety factor to consider. He did murder someone, after all."

For once, I was grateful for Pisano's hotheadedness. If he had insisted we go out on the record, O'Conner might have felt trapped by the cameras.

"Charging someone with murder isn't evidence that he did it," I said. "My client's clean except for one juvenile incident which, of course, the court can't consider now that Michael's an adult."

"Oh, I see," Pisano said. "We're supposed to overlook his armed robbery conviction."

I had anticipated this. "Another instance of overcharging by your office," I said. I opened my briefcase and pulled out the arrest report of Michael's juvenile case. "My client walked into a 7–11 with a toy gun," I said, "under the influence of drugs, and was stopped before he could get out the door. Your office called it armed robbery, but the juvenile court saw it for what it was. Michael went to a camp, not even CYA. He was put on a long probation for purposes of helping him get off drugs. That's the real heart of his problems." I pushed the arrest report across O'Conner's desk.

Pisano started to speak, but O'Conner cut him off. "Let me read this." When he finished, he handed it back to me, saying, "Hmph."

"My client has a problem with drugs," I said, seizing the advantage, "not violence. He has a loving family willing to put up their life's savings to bring him home where he can continue to receive psychological counseling."

"Bring on the violins," Pisano muttered, shifting restlessly in his seat. "May I remind the court that this drug-addled ex–armed robber is charged with murdering a state senator."

"Let me stop you there," O'Conner said. "The victim's identity is not really relevant. The value of a human life isn't measured by a person's prominence."

"That's true," Pisano said, "but this man was a public official who was assassinated—"

O'Conner held up an admonitory finger. "Counsel, as you well know, the People could have alleged special circumstances in this case if they believed they could prove Senator Peña's murder was related to his official capacity. Those circumstances were not alleged—"

"Our investigation is ongoing," Pisano said.

"Well," the judge replied, "I have to deal with what's before me. Special circumstances are not alleged."

"No doubt," I suggested, "because the People know their case is weak enough without going for the death penalty."

"Weak?" Pisano said incredulously. "We've got an eyewitness."

"You have a tentative make," I said. "Which reminds me, the defense will also be asking the court for an *Evans* lineup. My client's not your man, and a live lineup will prove it."

Pisano muttered, "We'll see."

"You must be pretty sure of yourself," O'Conner said.

"Or bluffing," Pisano added sourly. "Where was he the night Peña was killed?"

"You know better than to ask questions like that."

O'Conner said, "You still haven't talked numbers, Mr. Rios, unless you're serious about that $100,000 offer you made out there." His tone implied that I was not.

"Five hundred thousand dollars," I said, "and that's more than it's worth, given the decrepit state of the case against Michael. That's just to feed the frenzy out there."

"Jesus," Pisano said. "You can't be serious. Judge, you let him out on $500,000 and the court of appeals will writ you so fast, the ink won't have time to dry on the order."

I glanced at O'Conner. This was clearly the wrong thing to say. "You may not know this," O'Conner said tightly, "but I spent nine years as a writs attorney for the court of appeals. Not once in those nine years did we ever second-guess a bail disposition."

Pisano knew he had lost, so he went for broke. "Always a first time, Judge."

"I have considered the bail request," O'Conner said from the bench, "and based on discussion which I had with counsel in chambers, I will order bail. You'll get your chance to make your record," he said to Pisano, who had half-risen to his feet. "Bail will be set at $750,000." A murmur went through the crowded court. They didn't know the extra $250,000 was O'Conner's cover-your-ass money. "With a number of conditions," he continued. "Defendant will be released to his parents under the probation office's home surveillance program. He will be required to wear an electronic monitor at all times and he will be confined to the family home. He will continue to receive psychological counseling. He will refrain from the use of any drugs, including alcohol, and he will be subject to random drug checks to test for compliance. He will obey all laws and comply with any terms of any earlier probation. His bail status will be reviewed at the preliminary hearing which will be," he paused and glanced at his calendar, "in Division 59 before Judge Schrader. Now, Mr. Pisano."

"Tino," I called at the boy walking ahead of me on the sidewalk. He slowed, glanced over his shoulder, then stopped to wait for me. Approaching him, I noticed how little he resembled his father. It was his mother he favored. In his blue suit and red tie, he might have been a first-year associate at a big firm; in fact, I'd heard he was in law school, at Southland University, a bastion of the children of privilege. Apparently, Gus had seen to it that his son would be spared the deprivations he had experienced.

"Hello, Mr. Rios," he said neutrally.

"Call me Henry," I told him. "I just wanted to thank you for talking to Carolina Ruiz this morning."

This wasn't entirely true. I still itched about Michael's relationship to Angela Peña and although Michael's account had been plausible, I kept returning to Lonnie Davis's description of them. He was, after all, impartial, whereas Michael might well have something to hide. It had occurred to me that if he had killed Peña, and it involved Angela, he would have reason to lie about her, to protect her.

"That's all right," Tino said, relaxing. "I know it must be hard for her, having Mike in jail."

I was taken by the magnanimity of his tone. "Considering why Michael is in jail, you seem remarkably free of anger."

"Being mad at Mike's not going to bring my dad back," he said.

"But you want justice done, don't you?"

He looked uncomfortable. "Maybe I shouldn't be talking to you. I'll probably be a witness. I was there, you know."

"I'm not going to ask you anything about that night," I told him. "Can I walk with you for a minute?" Before he could answer, I took him by the elbow and started moving. "You're in law school, I hear, at Southland."

"Yeah, just started." We came to a red light.

"In September?"

He shook his head. "I transferred last quarter from Berkeley."

The light changed. "Where's your car?'

"Just around the corner."

"Boalt's a good school," I said. "Some would say better than Southland. Why'd you come back?"

"After my dad's—," he hesitated, "accident up in Sacramento, I wanted to be close to my family."

"I can understand that," I said, as we passed City Hall. "What did your parents think about Angela going out with Michael?"

He stopped. "I beg your pardon?"

"They knew, didn't they?"

"Excuse me, Mr. Rios," he said, politely, "but I don't think I want to talk to you anymore."

"I understand, Tino. Just doing my job."

"Sure," he said, and hurried away.

When I got back to my office, I went through the investigation reports on Peña's murder. Something Tino said had struck me as wrong. Sure enough, the report stated that only his mother and sister had been with Peña at dinner the night he was killed. Why had he lied? I called Freeman and asked him to check around, to see what he could find out about Angela and Michael, and on Tino's whereabouts the night of the shooting.

EIGHTEEN

As it happened, Michael didn't get out of county jail until the next morning because there was still the matter of his probation violation pending. Pisano had attempted to use the probation hold to keep Michael in jail until the prelim, but the judge who had imposed probation released him after conferring with Judge O'Conner. It was courageous of O'Conner to stand up for his bail decision; the media had slaughtered him for it. The district attorney, a tireless self-promoter, threatened to go all the way to the state supreme court to have the decision reversed. The city's other politicians all lined up behind him, each taking their shots at O'Conner. As a consequence, I was not feeling particularly well-disposed toward elected officials as I drove downtown to meet Inez Montoya for lunch.

On my way in, the phone rang. It was Freeman. "He was at school, in the library."

"Who?"

"Peña's son," he said. "He took a call around eleven."

A thick layer of smog lay in the air, dissolving the gleaming spires of downtown.

"Are you sure, Freeman?" I asked.

"Sorry to disappoint you," he said.

"Oh, well," I said. "It was just a thought." A man selling sacks of oranges at the intersection held one up and shook it hopefully in my direction. "What about the girl?"

"She was with her dad," he deadpanned.

"Yes, I know that. What about her and Michael?"

"She goes to that Catholic school out by the airport," he said, "but lives at home. She's got a couple of girlfriends, but as soon as I told them who I was, they clammed up. She does own a white Miata, though, if that helps."

"Anyone at SafeHouse remember seeing her with Michael?"

"The director, what's his name, Sweeny? Said he'd call the cops on me if I didn't clear out."

"I'll deal with him later," I said. "What about Tino's transfer from Berkeley? Was there any impropriety about it?"

"It checks out," he said. "I could go up there and ask around . . . " he said, dubiously.

"No, I don't think I could justify the expense. What about our gangbanger friend, Shorty?"

"Still looking," he said.

"Sounds like a washout on every front," I said.

"Well, here's something interesting," he said. "A couple of weeks before Peña got killed one of the neighbors called the cops on him."

"Why?"

"Domestic violence, it sounds like," he said.

"Any arrests?"

"No, cops came up, were told it was nothing and left. But," he continued, "I played a hunch and checked around the local hospitals. Mrs. Peña came in about three months ago, to St. Vincent's. Some bruises. Some bleeding." He cleared his throat. "She fell."

"Three months ago," I said. "That would've been after Peña's accident, after he supposedly sobered up. Who brought her in?"

"The boy," he said.

I drove into Little Tokyo where I was meeting Inez, and left my car in a new parking structure that had been put up on the site of a sushi bar I'd frequented when I'd first come to LA. Back then, only a couple of years earlier, the storefronts lining this section of First Street had been quaintly shabby, little restaurants displaying plastic replicas of food. Redevelopment had set in, however, and Little Tokyo looked glossier by the moment. I crossed the street and went into the Far East Café, the only Chinese restaurant on the strip.

She was waiting for me, in one of the enclosed wooden booths that lined the walls. A very old, very surly waiter slapped a greasy menu in front of me and asked me what I wanted to drink.

"A Coke," I told him. He twitched his nose in disapproval and scuttled off. "This is the worst Chinese food in town," I told her.

"My father used to bring me here," she said, shrugging. "Anyway, the almond chicken's not so bad."

"You wanted to see me," I said.

She smiled disarmingly, "You won't like me when I tell you, so why don't we order first."

The waiter returned with my Coke. Inez ordered, and he repeated each choice, muttering it caustically just under his breath, as he wrote it down.

When he left, she said, "We've been friends for a long time, Henry."

"This is going to be bad."

"Shut up and let me finish. I know I can talk frankly to you. Get off the Peña case."

This was brazen, even for Inez. "Why?"

"It's a bad career move, Henry. Look, the governor's anxious to appoint Latinos to the bench before the next election. He's been asking some of us for recommendations. Your name is on everyone's list. It won't be there for long if you insist on defending Gus Peña's killer."

"What happened to presumption of innocence?"

"This isn't law, this is politics." She dug a cigarette out of her purse. "You got the kid out on bail. You've done enough."

I looked at her for a moment, doing some political calculations of my own. "You going to run for Peña's senate seat?"

"What does that have to do with anything?" she asked, irritably.

"His widow's endorsement would be helpful."

"I represent the same district he did," she snapped. "I don't need anyone's endorsement."

"And of course, there's Peña's fund-raising machine," I went on. "Extremely efficient, from what I hear."

Our waiter rolled a trolley over and laid plate after plate of greasy, gray food on the table between us.

"And I don't need his money," she said.

"But that would help, too. Did the Peña family ask you to talk to me, or was it his money men?"

"When are you going to come in out of the cold, Henry?" She crushed her cigarette angrily. "You're Chicano, you're smart, you're articulate. You could do a lot of good for a lot of people if you'd come into the tent instead of standing outside pissing on it."

"Listen, I'm your biggest fan, Inez. I hope you do become mayor, governor, whatever you want, but I'm not interested in it for myself. I saw what that kind of power did to Gus Peña, I can see what it's doing to you."

"Do you? Well I have eyes, too, Henry. It's not the power you're afraid of. You're afraid of what people whisper about you behind your back because you're gay. Well, if you're so damn proud of it, why don't you fight for it? Take on the Peñas of the world. They don't think you're a man. Prove it to them."

"I've proved it to myself," I said. "That's all that matters."

"Oh, I give up," she said. "You're too fine for me."

"Inez, you don't mean that."

"Of course not." She ladled food onto her plate. "Eat, Henry. Some rice at least."

"No thanks," I replied. "I have to be at Parker Center at twelve-thirty for a lineup. Tell me something, Inez, did Gus beat the kids, too, or just Graciela?"

She picked up her chopsticks. "What makes you think I would answer a question like that?"

"Under the circumstances, I think you owe me," I said.

"Let's just say," she said, "he never left any visible marks."

I walked to Parker Center from the restaurant. Patrol cars moved in and out of the lot beside the police headquarters, and the sidewalk was stained purple where pedestrians had trampled jacaranda flowers fallen from a few spindly trees. Dusty stalks of birds of paradise opened their orange-tongued blossoms. The heat raised the smell of urine from all the dark little enclaves that the homeless used as toilets. A few of them trudged along the sidewalk with the government workers, conspicuous in ragged layers of clothes far too warm for the season.

I thought about Inez, gobbling lunch, and heading back to work to do the people's business. Yet for all her busyness, and that of the thousands of bureaucrats who filled the towers that surrounded me, the people did not appear to be better off. The only power any of us had was what we held in our hearts and minds, and in that respect, the bag lady squatting to piss on the lawn of City Hall was no different from Inez Montoya, or me.

I was standing in a narrow rectangle of a room, a couple of benches arranged to face a glass wall. Beyond the wall was a brightly lit platform and behind it, a wall marked with different heights. This room was not visible from the other side of the glass. I wasn't alone. I had lots of company, Detectives Laverty and Merrill, Anton Pisano, and a frail-looking man with a drooping moustache who'd been led into the room by two uniformed INS agents. Pablo Saenz, the People's star witness. He scrunched down in his seat, terrified by the authority arrayed around him. A very old man, with silky white hair, sat reading a paperback in the corner.

I had been studying the six-pack, the photo lineup from which Saenz had chosen Michael. It was a square piece of cardboard with six slots holding booking photos backed by more cardboard. The six men looked uniformly menacing, but there was little other resemblance except that all were Latino with the same basic facial structure, thin and narrow. That didn't bode well for this lineup; if Saenz had been able to pick Michael out of this group, then maybe he had seen him. Still, I was far from convinced his choice had been completely voluntary.

I approached him. "Where's the interpreter?" I asked Laverty. I didn't trust my Spanish.

"Why?" Pisano asked. "What do you want to ask him?"

"I'll have the questions and answers translated," I said.

The old man in the corner put his book down and said, in elegantly accented English, "I am the interpreter."

"I need you over here," I said.

He shuffled over, smiling, and bowing slightly. "At your service."

"Thank you, Mr. . . . "

"Sevilla," he said.

"I'm Henry Rios, the defendant's attorney. I want to ask Mr. Saenz a couple of questions."

Pablo Saenz had been listening to this exchange with mounting anxiety. I turned, smiled at him, and in my best, albeit faulty Spanish, said, "Mr. Saenz, I am a lawyer, and I have a few questions to ask you. Since my Spanish is not good, I will be asking through the interpreter, Mr. Sevilla. Please don't be nervous or frightened." He didn't look reassured.

Pisano, who had moved in, said, "What did you say to him?"

I repeated my remarks in English. "Now," I said to Sevilla, "ask him if the police showed him the photo lineup before he came here today?"

"Jesus, Rios," Pisano said, disgustedly.

Sevilla translated the question, having some problem with the concept of photo lineup, but eventually, he made himself understood. Saenz said, "No."

Sevilla repeated, "No."

"Ask him if either the police or the INS agents said anything at all to him about why he's here today, or what he's expected to do."

Sevilla translated. Saenz began to babble, but Sevilla cut him off, telling him to answer only yes or no.

"Wait," I told Sevilla. "This isn't a formal examination. Let him talk."

Sevilla apologized and asked Saenz what he was going to say before he had been stopped. I listened, able to translate that he had not been told why he was coming here, but only that if he cooperated he would soon be released.

Before Sevilla could translate, I said to him, "Ask him who said he would be released?"

Pisano said, "Wait a minute. What did he say before?"

"He said someone offered him a deal," I said. Then to Sevilla, "Go on. Ask him."

A moment later, Saenz was saying that the agents for *la Migra,* the INS, had told him they would release him as a reward for his cooperation with the police.

While Sevilla translated his answer, I debated whether I should ask him about the photo lineup, but to do so, it might be necessary to show it to him, and inadvertently refresh his recollection about Michael's appearance.

"That's all I have," I said.

"Then let's get this over with," Pisano said sourly.

Laverty came over and began reading to Saenz from a preprinted card that Sevilla translated, explaining the purpose of the proceeding. He was asked to look at the six men who were about to be brought out and say whether he recognized any of them as having been present the night of Peña's killing. He was cautioned that simply because the men were here was no indication that they had been present at the scene. He was asked if he understood. When he said he did, Laverty shouted, "Bring 'em out."

Six young Latinos, all about the same height and weight, all dressed like homeboys, in billowing khakis, sneakers, and plaid shirts over white T-shirts filed across the platform, as surly as models on a runway. Michael was the second from the right. Unlike the other men pictured in the photo lineup, these men bore a slightly closer resemblance to him. They glared and scowled into the glass, or feigned indifference. Michael stood stock still, looking straight ahead.

A minute passed, then two, then three. At five minutes, Pablo Saenz raised his hand and pointed, "*El.*" I followed his finger. He had chosen the man at the other end from where Michael stood. "*Tengo cierto,*" Saenz was saying. I'm certain.

I looked over at Pisano.

"How about two out of three?" he asked.

▲

CHAPTER

NINETEEN

▼

A COUPLE OF HOURS LATER, I WAS SITTING IN THE RUIZES' LIVING ROOM.
It was a big room in a big house, decorated with meticulous formal-
ity, less a home than a museum to hard-won affluence. Michael was
sitting at the far end of the same sofa on which I sat, yards of white
linen between us, his bare feet propped on the coffee table, eating
ice cream. In slacks and a white polo shirt, his hair greased down in
the fashion of the moment, he seemed the perfect, spoiled suburban
kid. From this distance, even the tattooed tear looked like nothing
more ominous than a mole.

Only the thick plastic band around his ankle ruined the effect.
Encased in the band was a device that sent a constant stream of
electronic signals to a VCR-sized black box at the other end of the
room. Somewhere, someone in the probation office monitored
bleeps on a screen that represented the circumference of Michael's
freedom.

Carolina came into the room, bringing me a glass of iced tea, a
sprig of spearmint tumbling jauntily over the side. She moved

around the room cautiously, as if afraid something might break.

"Get your feet off the table," she ordered Michael, as she set my tea down on an enamelled coaster. Michael ignored her and went on eating his ice cream. "Get. Your. Feet—"

He swung his feet off the table.

"Are you sure I can't bring you something to eat?" she asked me. We were good friends now, now that I'd brought her the news about the lineup.

"No, I'm fine," I said.

"What happens now?" she asked, sitting down, and lighting a cigarette.

"The preliminary hearing," I said. "The DA will try to go with what he's got, which may still be enough for the court to order Michael to stand trial."

She frowned. "But what about this lineup?"

"It weakens their case, but doesn't destroy it, entirely. Eyewitnesses make mistakes all the time. I imagine, if they decide to pursue the case against Michael, they'll ask Pablo Saenz to make a courtroom identification." I sipped the tea. "Even if he does identify Michael at that point, it won't have much value after today. I mean, his original ID was weak, and then today he couldn't identify Michael at all. After awhile, it starts to look like the prosecution's beating a dead horse."

"But they could still put him on trial," she said sharply.

"They could."

"Why?" she demanded.

"Maybe they don't have any better suspect," I said. "Maybe they still think he did it."

Michael's spoon clattered at the bottom of his empty dish.

"That's ridiculous," she said.

I didn't say anything. Michael hadn't said much to me after the lineup. What I really wanted was to talk to him alone.

"I wonder if I could speak to Michael alone for a few minutes," I said.

"Why?"

"Please," I said. "Just a couple of minutes."

She got up slowly from the chair, made a show of removing his ice cream dish and shuffled out of the room.

When she'd left, I turned to Michael and said, "OK, we're going to talk now. Who are you protecting?"

He looked at me. "I'm not protecting anyone. I told you before, I killed him."

"Michael, I don't believe you," I said. "What I think is that you're taking the rap for someone, but I don't know who. Now I understand what you're thinking. If we go to trial on this evidence, you expect to be acquitted, which is entirely possible, and then, not only will you be free, but whoever you're protecting will also be off the hook."

He watched me intently, but said nothing. He reached for his cigarettes.

"In fact," I said, "I think you expected what happened today. You expected it because you knew that you weren't there that night. But it was risky, Michael. The police got Saenz to identify you once, and they could have done it again." I paused to let this sink in. "We're probably lucky INS has had him all this time instead of the cops."

The door opened and Bill Ruiz came in, beaming. "Michael," he said, hurrying over to his son. "I heard what happened. Give your dad a hug."

Sullenly, Michael got up and let the big man enfold him.

"Thank you, Henry," Bill said. He walked over and shook my hand. "I guess we get to keep this place."

I smiled. They had put the house up to make Michael's bail.

"Where's my wife?"

"The kitchen," I said. "Michael and I were having a private talk."

"Sure, sure," he said. "It's great, really great." His face was anxious. "I guess I don't need to tell you how this has affected my business. Look, you two keep talking." He hurried out of the room.

Michael said, "I hope he fucking loses his business."

I studied him for a moment. "Maybe I'm wrong about your motives here," I said. "Maybe you want to go to jail to punish them."

He looked around the big room, its white furniture, tasteful wall-hangings, the good reproductions of pre-Columbian art nudging volumes of unread books on sleek bookshelves. A vase of gladiolus stood on the mantle over the fireplace. Next to it was a photograph of Carolina and Bill Ruiz dressed to the nines. Beside that was a picture of Michael, taken when he was three or four years old. There was no other evidence of his presence in the room.

"They want me in jail," he said, scowling. "Out of the way. Dead would be best."

"And what do you want from them, Michael?"

He shook his head. "Nothing. Not a fucking thing."

"You're eighteen," I said. "You could leave here, make your own life. Without drugs or booze. Without them. Just walk away from it."

"I don't know what you're talking about."

"Stop trying to get back at them by fucking up your life," I said. "Because sooner or later, you will end up dead. They'll get over it. Believe me, they'll get over it. And you'll be dead."

"I got plans," he said.

"Good, I'm glad to hear it. Of course, there's still the small matter of this murder charge hanging over your head. Now, if you weren't at the restaurant that night, you were somewhere else. Don't tell me you were at the park. Wherever you were, someone must have seen you, and could testify to it. With that testimony we can blow the case apart. Well?"

"They can't prove shit," he said, reverting to a homeboy drawl. "I don't have to say nothing."

That night I pored over every piece of paper I had that related to the Peña investigation: the official reports, Freeman's reports, my own notes. I was looking for a key to a door that I wasn't even sure existed, someone or something that would give me a different angle on this case. It wasn't until I re-read the notes of my first interview with the Ruizes that something caught my attention and held it. I called Edith Rosen, waking her.

"Edith, sorry to bother you, but do you know the name of Michael's grandmother, and where she lives?"

"Wait a minute," she said groggily. "I have to go to my desk."

I heard rustling, and then the yapping of a small dog. A couple of minutes later, she picked up a different phone.

"Somewhere," she said. "Oh, here it is. Got a pen? Maria Ruiz. Here's the address."

The front of her house lay in the shade of an immense pine tree, shaggy with dust, needles drifting through the hot air to a yard already deep in them, making a noise beneath my shoes like small bones breaking. Small dark birds winged between the branches. A red plastic ball was also lost in that tangle, tossed there by a child long ago.

The house itself was a two-story cottage, very old, like most things in this neighborhood which was too poor and too dangerous for the redevelopers. It was the kind of place you would have found in New England, delicate and elaborate, as if it had been spun in confectioner's sugar. I came to the dusty door and knocked, hard, the loud report echoing in the deep quiet of the place.

After a few minutes, an old woman opened the door. Her wispy hair was done up in a bun. She peered at me from behind thick-lensed glasses, her black eyes huge and wary. The flesh hung from her face in wattles, and a dark dress emphasized her shapelessness. In halting Spanish, I introduced myself. She invited me in and moved aside to let me pass.

She had me sit in the front room while she went back into the kitchen to bring us tea. I sank into a chair upholstered in deep maroon, resting my head on a doily. There was an oval portrait on the wall of a sailor that looked like it had been taken in World War II. The flags of Mexico and the United States flanked his expressionless countenance. Beneath the picture was a framed medal. The only other picture in the room was a large, bad oil painting of Jesus in the Garden at Gethsemane. At the front of the room was a new television hooked up to a VCR.

She shuffled back into the room, bearing a tray with a cup of hot tea and a plate of store-bought cookies. She put the tray on a small side table next to me, then laboriously pulled up a chair so we could talk.

I thanked her for the tea and cookies, complimented her house, and asked her about the sailor. He was her husband, she said, who had been killed at Iwo Jima. I expressed my regret at her loss, and she received this with the equanimity of someone who had been receiving such condolences for nearly fifty years. I drank some tea, ate half a cookie, and then said I wanted to ask her some questions about Michael.

"Ah, *si, mijito*," she murmured.

She nodded when I asked her whether he had stayed with her in the days before his arrest. Then I asked her whether he had been visited by a girl and a young man, about Michael's age, who had come in a small white car.

"*Pero, si,*" she replied, and added that they had come for him almost every day. He would leave with them for a few hours, and then return for dinner. Once they had stayed to eat, and they had both been well-mannered and respectful. "*Muy amables.*"

I asked her whether she had ever overheard them talking about a man named Peña. No, she said regretfully, she had only met them that once, and they had not spoken much more than to praise her cooking. They had eaten well, she added.

I drank more tea, ate another cookie, and then asked her why Michael had left.

She said the young man had come, without the girl, and talked to Michael for a long time. Michael had left with him, and he had not come back. It was only later, when she heard about his arrest, that she knew where he had gone. She was weeping. I held out a consoling hand and sat with her a few more minutes before getting up to leave.

She walked me out to the porch. How is he, she asked me, *mijito*. I told her Michael would be fine.

I drove away, thinking not of Michael but of the hours I had spent with Raymond Reynolds talking about my father. My father had been a man who, outwardly, was a respectful, responsible member of our small community, a collection of neighborhoods called Paradise Slough, the Mexican district of a town in northern California, Los Robles. It was not too different in spirit from Boyle Heights, the neighborhood I had just come from, a Spanish-speaking village in an Anglo city. Disdained by the majority, its people were tribal in their outlook and mores. Its cornerstone was the family, and in the family the father ruled, irrevocably and without question. Outside, in the larger world where they labored under the contemptuous eye of Anglo bosses, the fathers were social and political ciphers. No wonder, then, that in the families they tolerated no dissent from their wives and children. And they drank. They drank to wash down the slights they endured by day and to enlarge small lives which became heroic in alcohol-glazed rumination, but at their cores the fathers knew the full measure of their unimportance and, so, finally, they drank to quiet the rage.

But the rage would not be completely calmed. How could it? The church told them their reward would be in the next life, but this is small consolation for the back-breaking labors of the present, the years of enforced humility. When the rage exploded, they struck out at the only ones over whom they had any power: wives, sons, daughters, particularly the sons in whom they saw their own lost youths. The sons bore the blows and absorbed the rage. It was a recipe for patricide.

I knew this, it was in my blood, but only in talking to Raymond Reynolds had I realized that fifteen years after my father's death, I still bore a residue of the homicidal rage toward him. Seeing it in myself, I could now recognize its marks in other men whose childhoods had been similar to mine. Gus Peña, for instance, a powerful, angry man who tore through life as if he were stalking someone. His spectacular success had not been enough to break the circuits of resentment, any more than my fine academic degrees had, and we had both ended up like our fathers, seething alcoholics. There was a crucial difference though—I had not had a son to visit this fury on. He had.

Michael's room had been furnished by his parents' fantasy of what their son should be. The neat double bed was covered with a goose down bedspread, and on the wall above it was a map of the world, as if Michael had ever dreamed of going any place other than where drugs could take him. A rolltop desk sat unused in the corner. Bookshelves held only a few paperbacks, a baseball mitt cracked from disuse, and a tennis racquet in need of re-stringing. Michael sat on his bed in jeans and a black T-shirt, smoking a cigarette, watching me warily.

"I visited your grandmother this afternoon," I said. "'She told me you had had visitors while you were staying with her last time."

He made a show of tapping ash from the cigarette. "So what?"

"A boy and a girl who came in a little white sports car," I said. "Angela and Tino Peña."

He shook his head. "She's an old woman, she doesn't know."

I ignored him. "She knows what she saw, and now I know, too. It's time to tell the truth."

He leaned back, against the headboard. "I told you the truth, you just don't believe me."

"Michael, Tino killed his father. That makes him guilty of murder, but if you participated, if you helped him in any way, before or after, that makes you guilty, too, as an accomplice or a co-conspirator. Michael," I said, "you can't protect him anymore. He's going to jail. The only question is whether you're going with him."

He stared at me from behind a screen of cigarette smoke. His parents' voices drifted from down the hall. They were arguing, in Spanish. He took a drag from the cigarette, put it out. "I didn't know."

"You better tell me about it."

"Tino has a girlfriend, she was in the court."

"The one in gold lamé," I said.

He looked at me blankly. "Yeah, I guess, the blond one. She's like, thirty or something. His dad told him to break up with her. Tino said he would, but he kept going out with her. The old man found out about it and made him change schools and come back to LA."

"He met this woman in Berkeley? What was she doing down here?"

"She came with him. His dad beat the shit out of him when she showed up. He told Tino if he couldn't keep his dick in his pants, he would cut it off for him. He made the bitch go back up to Berkeley. After that, he kept his eye on Tino, checked up on him. Like, when Tino was studying in the library at night, his dad would call and make sure he was there."

"The woman came back," I said.

"Yeah, he rented her an apartment in Hollywood."

"Peña called Tino in the library the night he was killed," I said, "but it wasn't Tino who answered, was it? It was you."

"How did you know that?"

I didn't answer, wanting him to imagine I knew more than I actually did.

"Tino would tell the old man he was going to the library at night, then pick me up and drop me off there, while he went to screw his girlfriend. When the old man called, I talked to him."

"He must have recognized your voice," I said.

Michael snickered. "By that time of night, the old man was so drunk he didn't even know his own voice. I never said much, anyway. Mostly he just talked about what a great man he was, what a fine father, how much he sacrificed for his kids."

I remembered the night Peña had called my house and Josh had answered. Josh had also said Peña was so drunk he could hardly make out what he was saying.

"Go on," I told Michael.

He stubbed his cigarette into the ashtray. "Tino picked me up when the library closed at midnight and dropped me off, then he went home."

"What happened the day Peña was killed?"

"Tino called me and asked me to go to the library for him. So I went, you know. No big deal. But when he picked me up, he was, dressed down, you know, like a homeboy. It was real funny because Tino's particular about his clothes. And he wasn't driving his own car. He had this old beater."

"Did you ask him about it?"

"Sure," he said. "He told me he was playing a joke on his girlfriend. He said it was her fantasy to fuck a homeboy, so he was going to surprise her. I thought, whatever."

"And the next day you heard about Peña's murder and you figured it out."

"Later," he said. "Not right away, but I started asking him questions. Finally, he told me. And he told me I had to help him."

"Why?"

"Cause he said, if I didn't help him, he would claim I was in on it, too."

"Yes," I said, "I can see how he would say that, but you knew you were clean. Why didn't you just tell him to go fuck himself?"

For a moment, he didn't answer. He was staring at a picture inside his head and it was hurting. "For Angela," he said, finally.

"Angela knew." He looked at me, as if I could tell him why she had helped her brother kill their father, but all he said was, "She knew."

"Still, Michael," I said, softly, "even if you loved her, it's still your life you were risking, your freedom."

"I don't have any life without Angela," he said. "And Mr. Rios, she's pregnant. She's pregnant with my baby."

After a moment, I said, "So you were willing to risk prison for her by letting yourself get tried for Gus Peña's murder."

"It's no big deal," he explained wearily. "It's not like I got a life. She told me she would wait for me."

"And you have a record," I said, fitting together another piece. "For armed robbery. Did Tino know you had used a toy gun?"

He went red. "I couldn't tell anyone about that."

"So Tino assumed you'd used a real gun which, of course, made you an even better suspect in his father's murder." I looked at him, shook my head. "Maybe you thought you were helping Angela, but it was Tino you were doing the real favor for."

"For her, too," he insisted. "It's how I showed her how much I loved her. My baby girl. I can take care of her. Her old man was such an asshole to her."

"Did Peña know you were going out with her?"

"Fuck no. He would have killed me."

"When did you first start seeing her?" I asked, a thought forming in the back of my mind.

"She brought him to SafeHouse, and she, like, saw me, and remembered me from when she came here." He frowned. "She was pretty stuck up, but then, you know, she got to know me better. That's when it started. She's not stuck up, Mr. Rios. She's just real shy, really quiet." He said it as tenderly as if he was speaking to her. "She's my baby. My baby girl."

I was drawing my own conclusions about Angela Peña, and they weren't charitable. She had played on his attraction to her to bring him into the plot to kill her father, because anyone could see that Michael Ruiz was starved for love. He was dying for lack of it, and from the drugs he used as a substitute. He had been born not belonging, not in this room and not in this family. He had tried to win acceptance from the homeboys in his father's old neighborhood, but they had seen him for what he was: a suburban kid who had fried his brains on drugs, not the kind of survivor you needed to be to make it on the streets. The only place he had really belonged was at his grandmother's reliquary of a house, where he could be half-dead and no one minded.

And then Angela had come into his life, and had given him something even drugs had failed to provide him, someone seemingly weaker than himself whom he could take care of. I wondered whether it was she or Tino who thought up telling Michael she was pregnant. Tino, probably; he seemed to be the real moving force behind all of this, but it was hard to believe Angela was blameless. For a moment, I considered disillusioning Michael to enlist his cooperation in what I wanted to do next, but the way he had talked about her, I didn't think it would work. I took another tack. If I could persuade him she wasn't involved, he might not warn her that I knew.

"Michael, have you considered the possibility that Angela didn't know that Tino was going to kill their father?"

"What do you mean?"

"Look, Tino is the one with the problem. In his situation, I would use anyone I could to protect myself. Maybe even my sister."

He seized upon this, wanting to believe in her innocence. "You mean, like, he told her if she didn't talk to me, he would say she was in it all along?"

"Something like that."

"What a prick," he said. "He's the same as his old man. Wait until I tell her it's OK."

"Michael," I said, "do me this favor. Don't call her until I tell you it's all right."

"Why?"

"Because I'm going to try to talk Tino into turning himself in."

"Good luck, man," he said, genuinely alarmed for me.

CHAPTER

TWENTY

▼

I was waiting in my office for Tino Peña to keep our appointment. It was nearly seven. That morning, I had gone to Southland University where Tino went to law school—had gone to law school, rather, having dropped out two days after his father's funeral—and tracked down the student worker who had checked IDs at the law library the night Gus was killed. She had remembered the boy with the peculiar mole beneath his eye who had come in that night. Later, playing out a hunch, I'd called the vital records department at the Hall of Administration for Alameda County, where Berkeley was located, and confirmed Agustin Peña, Jr., and Jamie Starr had obtained a marriage license the previous December. Then, I'd dictated a long memorandum detailing every fact that connected Tino to his father's murder and left it in Emma's in-basket to be transcribed in the morning.

Now, as the time approached, I switched on the intercom button on my phone, connecting me to an office at the end of the hall where Freeman Vidor was waiting to listen in on my conversation with Tino. When I had told Freeman what I planned to do, he had urged me to call the police, and turn my evidence over to them. I had refused.

Tino Peña was not just a boy who had killed his father. He was my mirror and I wanted to look into him, and for him to look into me. I wanted to give him a chance to explain to me and himself why he had done it. He would need to know, for the long road ahead of him, not just to the inevitable trial, but also to the rest of his life.

I'd been thinking about the hidden law. The hidden law that takes us for what we are, and answers nothing when we lie. Gus Peña's life had been a lie, a whirlwind by which he sought to distract himself from the abiding sadness at his core. With his long El Greco face, he was a martyr to *machismo,* the tragic code by which his father and mine had lived, mistaking fearlessness for courage. They weren't the same, I knew that now. Courage requires hope. That's what I wanted to tell Tino, who had already demonstrated his lack of fear.

I heard footsteps coming up the hall, and then he was standing in the doorway. Looking at him, in jeans and a bulky Berkeley sweatshirt, his hair plastered down and gleaming, I saw the resemblance between Tino Peña and Michael Ruiz. I had missed it before, but before I hadn't been looking for it.

"Come in, Tino, have a seat."

The boy walked slowly toward me, and sat down. He said, "You said you had something to tell me about my dad's murder."

His eyes were watchful. His hands lay uneasily in his lap, pushed against something hard beneath the sweatshirt, tucked into his waistband. A gun.

"I understand you've dropped out of law school," I said.

It caught him off-guard and made him even more nervous. He said, "No, I'm just taking a quarter off. My mom needs me at home."

"What kind of law do you plan to practice?"

He relaxed. These questions were familiar to him. "I don't know," he said. "I'll probably go into politics."

"Like your father," I said. "You ought to be extremely successful, judging from the eulogy you gave at his funeral. It was very moving."

"Thanks," he muttered.

"It didn't seem odd until later, when I thought about it," I said. "You never once used the word 'love.'"

He stiffened. "You didn't hear right."

"No, I listened very carefully. You know, Tino, working on Michael's defense, I've learned a lot about your father. Everyone agrees he was a dazzling politician, but a hard man to know and a hard man to love."

"My father was the best," he said, passionately.

"The best father?" I wondered. "The best husband?"

"What do you want, Mr. Rios?" he asked carefully.

"The truth," I said. "I want to give you the opportunity to tell me the truth."

He shook his head slowly. "I don't understand."

"Let me tell you a few things about your father, and you add them up for me, OK?" Without waiting for a response, I said, "Your father was drunk when he died, Tino, even though he'd made a speech just a couple of weeks earlier claiming that he'd overcome his alcoholism. Even before then, after he'd killed that man in Sacramento, after he'd gone into SafeHouse, he sent your mother to the emergency room at St. Vincent's with a busted lip and a black eye. You drove her there."

He watched me intently, his dark eyes cold and hard, his hands pressing against his waist.

"And while he was at SafeHouse, he conducted business as usual, in violation of every rule of the house. He got away with it because SafeHouse depends on state money and he knew it. I think that's probably why he went there in the first place. Am I right?"

Almost imperceptibly, he nodded.

"It was all a show," I said. "Something for public consumption. In private, he hadn't changed at all. He still drank, he still beat your mother. He forced you to transfer from Berkeley to break up your marriage."

He opened his mouth in astonishment. "How did you—"

"A hunch."

The astonishment faded. Grimly, he said, "That punk talked."

"Not willingly," I said. "I went to visit his grandmother. She told me he had had visitors, you and your sister. She thought you were very nice. But that's always been your role, hasn't it, Tino? The nice boy, the obedient son."

"He'll get off," he said. "The eyewitness couldn't identify him in a million years."

"Because he wasn't there," I said. "I know. He was sitting in your carrel at the law library at Southland. The girl who let him in remembered the mole," I touched my face where Michael's teardrop was tattooed. "You're right. He'll get off, but that raises interesting questions about where you were."

"No one needs to know that."

"Don't you think the district attorney will be curious?"

He smiled. "My dad helped elect him," he said. "My wife will swear I was with her." His smile tightened. "Mike's not going to talk, is he? What does he care once you get the charges dropped?"

"And you're willing to live with it?"

He was too smart to answer. He sat back and grinned.

"You must have truly hated him."

"I don't think you want to say anything else, Mr. Rios. For your own good."

"I had a father like yours," I said. "Everyone thought he was a model family man because he provided for us, but no one knew what happened when the door was locked for the night. I never told anyone, either, not about the drunken rages, the beatings, the constant humiliation, because I didn't think anyone would believe me, and because I was ashamed at myself for not standing up to him. I carried those secrets most of my life, Tino, because I thought they were my secrets. But I was wrong. They were his secrets. I wasn't doing myself any favors. I was just helping him. That's how he continued to control me, even after he died. You think your life will be better because he's gone, but you're wrong. He's still calling the shots."

"I own my life now," he said.

I shook my head. "He took it with him when you buried him. How are you going to get it back?"

"Are you going to the police?" he asked, slowly. "Is that what this is all about?"

I chose my words carefully, mindful of the gun in his waistband. "The law is changing. It's beginning to recognize defenses that explain why someone who has been terrorized all his life might finally strike out."

"Premeditation," he said. "Lying in wait. That's special circumstances. That's the death penalty."

"If the entire family was involved," I said. "If they banded together, it would be hard for a jury to convict."

I saw doubt flicker in his eyes.

"There must be years of records," I said. "Emergency room records, reports of schoolteachers about a student who comes in with suspicious injuries, neighbors who remembered the arguments, who maybe called the cops. There's already a very public record of your father's alcoholism."

"They don't let you off," he said, looking at me very hard, waiting for me to lie.

"Not entirely," I said. "It's a classic second-degree plea. Fifteen years to life, two years for the gun. In nine years you'd come up for parole."

"Nine years," he said softly. "I'd be thirty-five." He shook his head, "And that's if you're right, but you can't promise anything."

"No, I can't. But ask yourself this, Tino, whose interests would be served by sending you to death row? Who would be calling for your blood? Your mother? She's the only one who would have the moral credibility to demand that you be prosecuted to the full extent of the law. But she won't do that, will she?"

"No," he whispered.

Because she *knew,* I thought. That's why she'd had Inez Montoya try to call me off, to protect her son.

"It's already a nightmare for your family," I said. "No one is going to want to make it worse."

He looked down at his hands, his shoulders trembling. When he looked up at me, he was crying. "I can't take the chance, Mr. Rios."

"It's your only chance, Tino." I drew a deep breath and played my last card. "Killing me will only make it worse. You might be able to live with your father's death, but not the death of an innocent man. Give me the gun, Tino."

Now he wept loudly, his body shaking. "I can't."

"You're not a killer, Tino," I said, hoping that Freeman would stay put. "Give me the gun, Tino. I can help you. I understand what it's been like. Kill me, and there won't be another chance to make peace with yourself. Give me the gun, now. Tino, give me the gun."

He pulled the sweatshirt up, revealing the butt of a .22, and pulled it out of his waistband, holding it in his hand. I forced myself to remain perfectly still, though my guts had turned to liquid, and my brain screamed, get down.

"Put it on the desk," I said.

He looked at me, then at the gun. We sat there for the world's longest minute, and then, slowly, he lay the gun on the desk, and pushed it toward me. Slowly, I reached out and took it, opened my desk drawer and dropped it in. Out of the corner of my eye, I saw Freeman standing at the doorway, tucking his own gun back into his holster. He moved back into the corridor.

I came around the desk and put my hands on Tino's shoulders. He hugged my waist and wept. I stroked his head, murmuring, "It's OK, son. It's OK. It's OK."

* * *

Much later, I sat in my office with the tape that Freeman had made of the conversation. I played it back, and after it finished I sat there for a long time, thinking about the price I had almost paid to give Tino a chance to finally be free of his father. My father would have called me a fool for taking the risk. But he would have been wrong, as he had always been wrong about me, so blinded by his notion of what it meant to be a man that he had never seen his son's courage.

I pushed the erase button.

▲

CHAPTER

TWENTY-ONE

▼

I STOPPED TAKING CASES AFTER TINO'S WHICH, AT ANY RATE, TOOK most of the summer to try. The DA went after him with special circumstances, but the case was only half-heartedly prosecuted. Day after day, the revelations of Gus Peña's private persona filled the news. By the time I began the defense, there were letters to the editor demanding to know why the family was being subjected to further suffering. The jury came back with a second-degree conviction. He was sentenced to fifteen years to life in the medium security prison at San Luis Obispo. I went up to visit frequently the first few weeks he was there. So did Edith Rosen, who had gone into private practice.

SafeHouse closed its doors shortly after the trial ended, pending an investigation by the state arising from testimony about Gus Peña's stay there. Last I heard, Chuck Sweeny was trying to open a place in Nevada.

Michael's probation was violated in his armed robbery case and he was sentenced to the California Youth Authority until he turned twenty-one. Angela Peña was not, as it turned out, pregnant. The Ruizes settled their bill with me promptly, and that was the last I heard from them.

Inez was elected to fill Gus Peña's unexpired term in the state senate.

By the end of August, I had finished my last case. I closed up my practice, helped find Emma another job, and went home.

Summer was over. I could feel the change of season in the slight chill beneath the breeze that blew through the sycamores on the quiet side street in West Hollywood. I walked slowly, letting the breeze curl around my chest, and thought of Lonnie's fingers tracing the plate of my torso as we lay in bed watching the light deepen in his room where I had spent the previous night. I didn't delude myself into thinking that being with him meant anything more than it did, but it was enough. When I wasn't with him, I was spending time with Eric and Andy in Santa Barbara, trying to remember what it had been like when I was eighteen and the world had laid its possibilities at my feet.

I came to the front of an apartment building, searched the directory for Josh's name, and when I found it, called up on the security phone.

"Henry?" he asked.

"Hi."

A buzzer sounded and I pushed the door open. I rode the elevator up to the third floor and he was standing on the breezeway, waiting for me, relaxed and comfortable in blue sweatpants and a yellow tank top. I hadn't seen him since May. For a time, he hadn't even called, and I'd had to let that go. Then, yesterday, he had asked me to come over. Seeing him, all the sadness came back, and all the regret. He walked toward me, grinning, and hugged me, then led me into the apartment he shared with Steven.

"This is very nice," I said, observing the polished surfaces of the expensively furnished room.

"Yeah," he said, "not bad for two guys on disability. Most of it's Steven's," he added, seriously. "Souvenirs of when he was a junior executive at a studio. They dumped him when they found out he had AIDS. Actually, he lives off the settlement money from his lawsuit against them. Do you want something to drink?"

"Mineral water?"

He ducked into the kitchen and reappeared with two glasses of mineral water. "Your cocktail."

He sat down beside me, put his hand on my leg. "You look great, Henry."

"You, too," I said, tracing a bulging biceps. "You've been working out."

"I've got lots of time to spend at the gym."

"What about school?" I asked him. When we broke up, he had been in his last quarter at UCLA.

He sipped his Calistoga. "I had to drop out." He tapped his head. "The mind is going."

"What do you mean?" I asked, smiling, ready to play along.

"I've lost about ten percent of the use of my brain already. The other day at dinner I couldn't remember the word for salt."

I stopped smiling. "This isn't funny."

"I'm not joking," he replied.

I started to cry. He put his arm around me, and let me sob against his chest, hard and muscular now from lifting weights, the chest of a beautiful young man with fifty years ahead of him. He stroked my hair and called me by the small names he had invented for me while we lived together. After a few minutes, I pulled myself together and leaned back into the sofa, wiping my face with my hands.

"It's not fair."

He sighed, drank some mineral water. "There are some things I need to take care of while I still can. I need a will, Henry."

"That's why you asked me to come, about your will?"

"Not just that, but to tell you. To ask for your help."

"Anything."

"Let's start with a will. There's not much. My grandfather set up a trust for all us kids, and I have a few stocks, that sort of thing. I want it to go to AIDS organizations, to Act Up and a couple of other places. I know you've been doing wills for PWAs for a couple of years."

"I never thought I'd do yours."

His expression was complex. "I guess we were both kind of living in a fantasy. You thought if you didn't let me grow up, I wouldn't ever die. I thought you were strong enough to do it."

"I never meant to keep you from growing up."

"I know that," he said, with a trace of the asperity of our last days together. Then, more gently, he added, "It was the only way you knew how to take care of me, by being the grown-up for both of us."

"I'm sorry, Josh."

He looked at me for a moment. "I think you'd do it differently now."

"Yes, I think you're right."

He got up and walked over to a desk, returning with a folder. "I've written out what I want, basically. I thought you could take this and put it into legalese."

I opened the folder. He had filled pages with his sloping backhand. "Yes, I can do that."

"I want to be cremated, Henry," he said, "My parents won't like it, but if you tell them it's what I wanted, they'll respect it. And I want my ashes divided up into five parts, one for them, two for my sisters, one for Steve—if he's still around—and one for you. Take them someplace that was special to us."

The only way I was going to get through was simply to respond to what he was saying without thinking about it.

"OK, what about a service?"

"At the church where Cullen's was," he said. "It's memorial service central anyway. I guess no one will mind that I'm a Jew."

"There's the gay synagogue."

He grinned. "Let's do it my way, OK?"

"Sorry."

"I know this is hard for you, Henry. There isn't anyone else I can talk to about it without breaking down myself. There's a song I want them to play, from that opera you dragged me to the last time we were in San Francisco. By Gucci."

"Puccini," I said. "*Suor Angelica.*"

He nodded. "Where she sings about her baby in heaven. It made my heart stop."

I remembered. *Ah! dimmi quando in cielo potro vederti? quando potro baciarti!*

"'When shall I see you in heaven? When shall I kiss you?' You're going to make me cry again."

"There will be enough time for that later, Henry," he said, gently. "Have you been seeing anyone? I don't like to think of you alone."

"I haven't been."

He smiled. "Well, tell me about him."

"Josh . . . "

"I want details, Henry."

"OK, his name is—"

I couldn't sleep that night, so I got out of bed, carefully, not wanting to wake Lonnie. I went into the living room and opened the windows to the cool air. I found the CD of *Suor Angelica* and put it into the player. I sat on the floor beneath the window, skipped the disc to the right place, pushed the play button and waited for the music to begin.